IMAGINE NATION

By Caiden Hooks

IMAGINE NATION

By Caiden Hooks

Paperback ISBN: 978-1-961993-44-0
HardcoverISBN: 978-1-961993-45-7
Ebook ISBN: 978-1-961993-46-4
LCCN: 2025922418

For MaKenzie, my Love, who loves reading and learning, and for all those who know (or are willing to learn) the value of pure imagination.

Identifiers:
Paperback ISBN: 978-1-961993-44-0
HardcoverISBN: 978-1-961993-45-7
Ebook ISBN: 978-1-961993-46-4
LCCN: 2025922418

Available in paperback, hardback, and e-book

Scripture quotations are taken from the *Legacy Standard Bible* (LSB), © The Lockman Foundation. Used by permission. All rights reserved. The Lockman Foundation also produces the *New American Standard Bible* (NASB). *The Legacy Standard Bible* is distributed through Three Sixteen Publishing.

The acronym O&M used in this book refers to orientation and mobility, a type of navigation training essentials to blind and visually impaired individuals. Training in this field, along with many other independent living skills for blind young adults, is offered by **the Summer Orientation & Mobility and Adaptive Living Resource program**, offered by LH Bindustries. SOAR is their program. For more information, visit https:// lhbindustries.com/soar/

Now I, Paul, myself plead with you by the gentleness and forbearance of Christ—I who am humble when face-to-face with you, but courageous toward you when absent. But I beg that when I am present I need not act so courageously with the confidence that I consider to daringly use against some, who consider us as if we walked according to the flesh. For though we walk in the flesh, we do not war according to the flesh, for the weapons of our warfare are not of the flesh, but divinely powerful for the tearing down of strongholds, as we tear down speculations and every lofty thing raised up against the knowledge of God, and take every thought captive to the obedience of Christ, and are ready to punish all disobedience, whenever your obedience is fulfilled.

2 Corinthians 10:1–6, Legacy Standard Bible

PROLOGUE
THE POWER of the PAGE

"And so," the councilman said, his arm gestures straining his ill-fitting gray suit, "it behooves the village to cease spending much-needed funds on a project which is, by our estimation, neither necessary nor sustainable."

"Thank you, Mr. Beaumont," Mayor Hegseth replied, adjusting his red bow tie. "Mrs. Davis, your closing statement, please."

"Thank you, Mayor," Ema Davis said, straightening, catching herself smoothing her wavy brown hair, and lifting her chin. "Fair people of Odessa, I urge you not to dismiss the importance of Imagine Nation—both for this community and for what it represents. My father founded this bookstore when the internet was in its infancy, because he loves reading and believes in the power it gives those who practice it. Today, yes, we have devices that can simulate entire worlds around us—but they tend to isolate us rather than unite us.

"Imagine Nation has always been a place where people of all ages, especially young people, can gather to connect, learn, create, and grow. As parents, would you rather see your child shut away in their room, immersed in a screen that cuts them off from the real world—or discovering new worlds that enrich their education and worldview? If the former, then by all means, shut Imagine Nation down. But if not, then let us begin writing a new chapter—not only in the store's history, but in the story of our village and in the lives of our children."

CHAPTER 1

THE WORLD WITHOUT WALLS

The desert town lay scarred and burning before him, the sound of rifle and artillery fire ringing in his ears. He scanned the horizon, searching for enemy fighters, the grip of his weapon tight in his right hand.

"Zech?"

His laser targeting sight swept up and down the sand-colored wall of the building in front of him. "Where are you, *little mujes?*" he muttered.

"Zech?"

Just then, his optics lit up. Quickly, he checked his diagnostic pop-up display. Not a friendly. "Jackpot." He tightened his grip on his weapon—

Suddenly he heard a scream from behind him: *"ALLAHU AKBAR!"* and gunfire erupted behind him. Reflexively, he clamped down on the trigger—

"Zechariah Forshaw!"

A sharp pain yanked at his scalp as the sounds of Iraqi street combat vanished.

"What?" he snapped, looking up sharply, rubbing

his tousled, copper curls where the headset had caught them. "Mom! What're you doing?!"

"I've been calling your name for the last five minutes!" his mother snapped, wiping sweat from her flushed forehead. "I want you to take out the garbage."

"No," he groaned.

"It needs to be out there tomorrow."

"I'll do it later, okay?"

"Well, how about your homework?"

"Fine," he muttered with a shrug.

Her hazel eyes narrowed. "You're at a C or lower in everything but lifting. You've got a D-plus in math! Are you even doing your work?"

Zech shrugged again. "Sure."

His mother fixed him with a long, stern glare. "Over half your teachers say you're missing work. Even Coach Limbaugh is worried about you!"

"H-yeah! Why would *he* care? He's the strength and conditioning coach, not a teacher!"

"Zechariah!" Now she was skewering him with a fiery stare. "You can't participate in sports or other clubs if your grades keep falling! And if you aren't doing your schoolwork because you're messing around blasting *jihadis* in Kabul—"

"Mosul."

"I don't care!" His mother's voice shot up to an exasperated scream. "If you put half as much energy into your classes as your combat missions—"

"I'll be fine, Mom! I don't wanna be like Corban and become valedictorian or anything! I just need to graduate!"

For a moment, his mother's face flushed an even deeper crimson, and she opened her mouth as if to speak. But she said nothing, choking on the number of things that she wanted to say. Then her face hardened into stony resolution. Quick as lightning, she reached over to the wall above his desk where his video game console sat, yanked the power cord from the outlet, and scooped up the device, and turned to leave.

"That's not the point," she said sternly, whisking the trailing cords up into her arms as she went. "You can have this back when you finally understand that." With that, she freed one hand and shut his bedroom door firmly behind her.

Zech stared numbly for a moment: first at the door, then at the empty spot on the desk where his console had sat only seconds before, then at the stack of games he could no longer play. Then a raw, rampant, red-hot rage surged through him—scalding like boiling water in his veins. *How dare she do this to him!* With a furious yell, he punched the wall as hard as he could. The drywall gave way with a *crunch,* and he blinked, stunned, at the fist-sized hole he'd just made.

Quickly he darted to his closet, found an old shoebox from the last Christmaskah (Christmas/Hanukkah) get-together, and tore off the lid. Flattening out the cardboard, he tacked it over the hole, then stood back and surveyed his work.

Not great, but passable—for now.

Ever since his father had left him, his mom, and his older brother for his stock exchange secretary, their decreased income had hit his family hard. *No need for her to shell out the money to fix it now,* he told himself. *Besides, how's it any of her business anyway? She's meddled enough!*

With that thought, a cruel idea slithered into his head. Going to his bedside, he knelt down, rummaging through the heap of books and crumpled papers spilling from his backpack. Eventually, he found what he was looking for: a red Sharpie. A flash of guilt mixed with satisfaction flickered through him as he remembered taking it from his tenth-grade math teacher last year—the pen she'd used to mark so many of his answers wrong.

Sharpie in hand, he approached the cardboard and, sneering to himself, drew a crude thumbs-up, then added an arrow pointing to another unmistakable hand gesture. Inside the outline, he scrawled: "THIS IS WHAT THAT MEANS IN IRAQ!!!" They were rough—not only because he was not the best artist, but because he was drawing on an upright surface and leaning over his desk. Still, he figured it got the point across just fine. Smirking with grim satisfaction, he returned the Sharpie to his bag, then sighed and pulled out his homework. Dropping into his chair, he started working—sulky, but resigned.

CHAPTER 2

AWOL

"You're joking!" Eddie Longshore whisper-yelled as Mrs. Davis spoke from the front of the room. "She really did *that?*"

"Yup," Zech said furtively, gesturing for Eddie to tone it down.

"So what did you do?" Eddie asked, lowering his voice.

"I . . . made her a little sign to show her how I felt," Zech said with a smirk, suppressing his guilt with a touch of smugness. *"And,"* he added with a grin, "it's from another culture, so she'd like it—if she *cared!"*

"Nice! Got a pic?"

Zech scrolled on his watch and showed it to his friend.

Eddie snorted. "Bro, that's awesome! Although the resolution on the watch sucks."

"Yeah, but Mrs. Davis never confiscates watches," Zech said with glee, then snorted. "She's so old-fashioned! She spends so much time nerding out about Bible stories and stuff that she doesn't stop to think about the difference between a smartwatch and the kind her grandfather probably wore."

"For real?"

"We go to synagogue at her house. I should know. She doesn't even notice when the kids are obviously playing on their watches—so obvious a drugged *monkey* could figure it out—the *shlemiel*."

The two of them lapsed into soft snickers—until a sharp kick to both their chairs brought them up short. Whirling around, they saw Christie Cunningham glaring daggers at them through her glasses. "Shush!" she hissed.

"Mind your own business!" Zech shot back.

"I'm trying," Christie said through clenched teeth.

"Is everything all right, you three?"

Immediately they froze. Mrs. Davis was watching them with a curious expression.

"No, no!" Zech and Eddie said one after the other. Out of the corner of his eye, Zech saw Christie still glaring, but he ignored her.

Mrs. Davis studied them a moment longer, then said, "All right then," and went back to teaching.

Teacher's pet, Zech thought to himself. *If she doesn't like it, you'd think she could've found a seat closer to the front earlier in the year. But she's later to class than we are! Little hypocrite!*

English class was always a drag for Zech. He didn't know anyone besides Christie and Mrs. Davis who actually cared about the book they'd been assigned—whatever it was. Maybe *Moby Dick*? Finally, the bell rang, and he shot up to leave.

"Zech?"

He froze, his backpack halfway up his arm, just about

to sling it over his shoulder. "Mrs. Davis?" he asked, trying to keep his voice steady.

"May I have a word with you? I'll give you a tardy slip in case you end up being late on my account."

Zech considered. Even though he hated being in that room longer than necessary, he supposed he couldn't exactly refuse her. Besides, a tardy slip would certainly help; he'd finally have an excuse for being late. "Sure," he said, setting his bag on his chair.

"Thank you."

Mrs. Davis walked past him and shut the door, then turned back. Feeling a little awkward, Zech faced her. To his astonishment, his English teacher was looking at him with genuine concern. He did his best to hide his shock, though he was sure he'd blinked.

"Is everything all right, Zech?" she asked, her voice edged with worry.

Confused, Zech nodded. "Yeah. Why?"

"I'm just worried about you," Mrs. Davis said, and to his chagrin, Zech found it hard to doubt her. "You've peaked at seventy-five, and some of your homework packets are incomplete. Is everything okay at home?"

"Yeah! I'm fine, really!" Zech was surprised by the vehemence in his own words.

Mrs. Davis studied him for a long, uncomfortable moment, as if searching for a lie—or a hidden truth. Finally, she nodded. "All right, if you say so. Here." She walked briskly to her desk, scribbled something on a tardy slip, and handed it to him. "Sorry to keep you. Have a nice day!"

"Thanks," Zech muttered, leaving quickly, trying to ignore the way her words tugged at him.

* * *

"All right, listen up, gents!" Coach Brent Limbaugh barked, turning to face the class with his back to the weight racks. He ran his fingers through his graying beard. "Some of you yahoos can't seem to keep your grades above water." Several students, including Zech, stared blankly at him. "You're at a C or lower. And I just wanna say that I'm sick an' tired of it! You are not at Odessa High just to sling these bars around, although—that's fun too. You are here to *learn*, first and foremost! And if you're not willing to shoulder your academic responsibilities, then you can walk your happy be-hind outa my weight room *right now!* Am I understood?"

Nobody moved.

"Actually, ya know what?" Coach's cheeks flushed. "I had a list of some people here I'd be *willing* to kick outa my class till they straighten out, just in case you had less mettle in ya than these bars. You, Forshaw!"

Zech's heart dropped as Coach pointed sternly at him.

"S-Sir?" Zech stammered.

"You wanna make somethin' of your life, son?" Coach barked, spittle flying.

"Y-Yes, sir!" Zech said, not quite sure this was

happening. "B-But I don't need to be *valedictorian* or anything, do I? Otherwise I wouldn't have time to be here."

He knew at once it was the wrong thing to say, as Coach's face flushed a deep purple, and for a horrible moment, Zech feared the older man might have an aneurysm. *"Out!"* Coach bellowed, jabbing his finger at the door.

"What?"

"Out! *Now!* And don't darken my door again until you understand how absolutely idiotic that statement was! Now *get—out!"*

Stunned, Zech turned and left, head drooping. He felt numb as he entered the locker room and changed back into his regular clothes. Only when he reached for his second sock did the weight of what had happened hit him like a medicine ball to the gut. He'd just been kicked out of his favorite subject— over *grades!* Anger welled up like a breaker at high tide. None of it made sense. Had his mom actually contacted Coach? She didn't even know him! *She better not have!*

He sat, fully dressed, for about five minutes, still trying to figure out what to do. He dared not tell his mother—or Eddie—and if Christie Cunningham ever found out, he'd be a dead man. His only choice was to act like nothing had happened. But then, he *couldn't* just sit there until the end of the period. He couldn't bear the thought of his former classmates whispering about him when they came back to change. *But can I slip away, toward my next class, without being seen?*

Slowly, quietly, he slipped on his backpack and crept out of the locker room, treading heel to toe. Looking toward the weight room, then down the corridor, he turned away, trying to appear casual. *I'm just heading to the bathroom between classes. Nothing suspicious about that.*

Just as he considered ducking into a bathroom to make his act more convincing, he collided with someone. Startled, he froze, only now realizing how far he'd walked. He was already halfway through the building, right in front of the library, its two wooden doors propped against the polished wooden frame. And there, glaring at him with books scattered at her feet, was Christie Cunningham.

"Oh, it's you," they said together, still shaken from the collision.

"What are *you* doing here?" Zech fumbled.

"Just grabbing some books for a research project for Mr. Johnson's AP World History class—like a *normal* person," Christie said icily. "What are *you* doing? Isn't this your gym period?"

"Lifting," he said automatically. Then dread gripped his chest. "And yeah," he added, scrambling, "but I—" He racked his brain for a believable lie. Then he had it. "It was just evaluation stuff today."

Christie raised an eyebrow, and to his chagrin, Zech liked it when she did. "Evaluation?"

"Yeah," he said, gaining confidence. "They have you do some exercises at the start of the year—high jumps, frog jumps, stuff like that—to see what you're capable of. I was up quickly, so I got to leave early. As he congratulated himself on covering his tracks, something dawned on him. "Wait, you're getting *books* for research? Why not just use a computer or something?"

Christie shrugged. "Just preference, I guess."

"What, you're not a normal person about *research?*" he teased.

She glared, fiery-eyed.

Zech smirked, taking this as a win, and mimed a phone with his thumb and pinky. "Yeah, the 1850s called; they want their poster child back."

To his surprise, Christie only shook her head. "Personally, I think people back then were a lot smarter about some things than *we* are," she said, smiling enigmatically, a strange mix of sadness and disappointment on her face. Then her smile grew as she gathered her books. "And anyway, telephones hadn't even been invented yet." With that, she turned on her heel and walked away down the hall, leaving him fuming and confused.

* * *

Zech's frustration simmered as he rode the bus home. Normally he'd have drowned out the day with a virtual reality campaign, but now that was part of the problem. All he could think about was getting to his room before his mom came home from the hospital. At this thought, his chin sank. The image of his mother at the reception desk—head down, eyes red and baggy, bracing for the next call, the next bill—or, worse, his antics—stirred long-hidden guilt. She didn't deserve that. And if she ever found out about the obscene sign—his gut lurched at the thought—she'd have his hide! He clenched his fists and began counting the stops. *Come on, come on! Hurry up!*

Finally, after what felt like forever, the bus stopped at the end of his block. Zech snatched his things and ran home. *No car in the driveway.* Relief loosened his chest.

Home alone!

Darting through the open garage, he burst inside, sprinting for his room—only to skid to a halt. Someone was standing right in front of it.

CHAPTER 3

TROUBLE ON THE HOME FRONT

Zech's eyes widened at the sight of his mother blocking his doorway, hands planted firmly on hips, her face white with anger. He was so stunned—and frankly terrified—that he didn't know just what to say. To his own consternation, he blurted, *"You're* home early," and immediately wished he could take it back.

"End-of-quarter party at work," she said curtly. "But I left early, and since Leslie wanted to stay, Corban dropped me off on the way to Olivia's." She held up her right hand. Zech's heart sank at the sight of his crude drawing. Evidently his face betrayed him, because she quickly lowered the cardboard and gestured over her shoulder into the room. "Come on," she said, almost lightly.

Slowly, hesitantly, dreading every moment, he followed her in. She pointed to the hole in the wall behind his desk. He couldn't bring himself to look at it, though she waited as if she expected him to. A heavy silence hung in the air between them, until she finally turned back to him—and his relief vanished when he saw her face again.

"Now, I'm hardly surprised," she said, her tone so level

it scared him more than shouting would have. "I've seen what you're like when you don't get your way. You've just gotten better at hiding it." She gestured at the posters on the walls—then, without warning, tore one down, revealing a slightly concave patch that Zech knew concealed an old repair.

"Your father used to patch them up," she said, her tone snapping slightly at his name. "I figured you'd outgrown this. But then I come in here and find *this?*" She brandished his cardboard sign, then drew two long breaths, recomposing herself. "You're paying for this," she said, hands back on her hips, her tone leaving no room for debate.

Zech said nothing. Why bother? He'd been caught.

"Why'd you come in running?" she asked, almost conversationally, though he knew better.

Still, he said nothing.

"What? Did you think you could hide this before I got home?" She gestured at the wall and waved the sign again.

"You didn't wash your hair today?"

Zech winced. "Didn't lift," he mumbled.

"What?"

"I didn't lift!" he half-shouted, cheeks burning.

Her eyebrows rose. "Why?"

He dropped his head. "I don't wanna talk about it."

She studied him for a moment, then nodded. "You mouthed off to Coach, didn't you? Got thrown off the team? You've made your bed with your grades and your attitude, and now you've—"

"Shut up!" he exploded, making her flinch. "Shut *up!* I

blew it! I'll admit it! Happy now? I *told* you I'm not Corban—summa cum laude, valedictorian, yada yada yada—and I *told* you I don't *wanna* be! At least Dad and Jessa don't care how bad I am in school, whatever they said before they up and left. And . . . and I wish he'd taken me *with* them!"

His mother's face flushed terribly, eyes opening wide, then crumpled. Then, arching her brow, she strode to him and slapped his cheek sharply. Without another word, she walked out of the room.

* * *

Ema Davis watched as the congregants shuffled out of New Harvest Messianic Synagogue, known to Odessa as hers and Jonathan's house. Her husband's sermon had been wonderful—as always—and teaching the children was as fun as ever. But as the house emptied, she noticed Joanna Forshaw hunched in one of the cushy armchairs in the living room.

"Joanna?" Ema asked, approaching her friend. "What's wrong?"

Joanna twitched, looked up briefly, then hid her face again, her reddened eyes concealed.

Something dawned on Ema. "Where's Zechariah? I didn't see him today."

Joanna sniffed, then finally looked up. "He came," she said flatly, holding herself together by sheer will. "He left with the Petersons."

Ema nodded, remembering the Forshaws' next-door neighbors. They had often chipped in since Darren fled to New

York City; this was hardly the first time they'd helped with carpooling. But Joanna looked troubled.

"Is Zech doing well?" Ema asked cautiously. "I talked to him yesterday after class, and apart from his grades he *seemed* okay, if a bit tense. Is everything all right at home?"

To her horror, Joanna broke. She burst into tears, curling into a tight ball and rocking so hard she slid off the chair onto the floor. Even as Ema tried desperately to comfort her, even when she offered tea minutes later, Joanna kept her face hidden, her carefully constructed dam of stoicism washed away in a torrent of tears. Out of the corner of her eye, Ema saw her husband watching with compassion and quiet faith in her. *O Lord God, help me!* she prayed.

At last Joanna calmed down somewhat, and Ema repeated her question: "What's wrong, Jo?"

"What's wrong?" Joanna asked ruefully. "I'm a failure of a mother, that's what."

Ema's jaw dropped. "What're you *talking* about? You're one of the strongest, hardest-working people I *know!*"

Joanna shook her head, tears streaking her flushed face. "I'm at the end of myself. I don't know what to do with Zech. He won't take school seriously—I took away his VR station; he lost his PE. Yesterday he disrespected me and said he'd rather be with Darren and Jessa and—"

"What?"

"—and I slapped him, because I couldn't say anything else—literally *couldn't!*—and then I ran!" A sob escaped her. "I ran from my son, because somewhere along the line I lost him, and I don't know how to get him back!"

She cried for a few more minutes, and Ema draped an arm over her shoulders and rocked her gently. Eventually, Joanna sniffed, her voice low and miserable: "I think I tried so hard to be his father that I failed at being his *mother*. That's where I lost him." Then her chin shot up. "I hate you," she snapped. Ema jumped back. "I hate you, Darren!" She spat on the floor and ground it in with her heel. "I know it's not right, but I hate you for what you've done to us, Darren Forshaw, you no-good, adulterous son of a . . . I'm sorry." Her chin dropped, her tone softening. "I just don't know what to do."

Ema had no advice. What Joanna needed wasn't words, but comfort. So she held her, and later drove her home. When Ema returned, Jonathan was waiting. With a weary sigh, she fell into his arms.

"I'll admit, honey, I'm lost," she said. "I'm no good at raising children, especially troubled ones!"

"You've got Christie," Jonathan said, stroking her hair.

"I'm her godmother," Ema reminded him. "And she's a star! Don't get me wrong, I love her, but it's just not the same." She sighed. "I certainly wouldn't know what to do in Joanna's shoes."

Jonathan smiled. "I have an idea. Your dad is great with these sorts of things. I bet if we asked him, he'd have some ideas."

Ema nodded, then blinked. "Yes, he *is*! He could be a kindred spirit for Zech."

Jonathan nodded. "And he'll need help getting the storefront ready for the grand reopening."

Ema beamed up at him, "That's a great idea. I'll tell Joanne in the morning."

CHAPTER 4

IMAGINE NATION

"Hey!" Eddie whisper-yelled across the empty space between them. "You okay, dude?"

Zech ignored him, staring at a point somewhere between his seat and the screen at the head of Mrs. Davis' classroom.

"Psst, hey!" Eddie tried again. "What's up, bro?"

"Nothing," Zech mumbled, still not looking at him.

Eddie frowned. "You sure you're okay, man? You're never this quiet—"

"Just shut up, Eddie," Zech snapped, then, softening with guilt, added, "Just leave me alone."

The hurt on his friend's face was instant, and Eddie turned away, resigned. The guilt in Zech flared inside him like oil in a hot pan. Quickly he stood, grabbed his backpack, and hustled out, making a beeline for the bathroom. Inside a stall, his mind circled back to all that had happened since Thursday evening. But at the center of it all was his mother's face—first white with rage, then flushed and wide-eyed, then crumpled. He hated when her face looked like that. He hated it. He hated her. *Stupid! How dare she!*

It was the scariest, saddest sight he'd ever seen.

The bell rang, and he hiked his bag on his shoulder to leave—then remembered he no longer had lifting. His shoulders slumped. So he stayed hidden until the hall emptied. No one came in to disturb him, and when the second bell rang, he peeked out, then stealthily made his way into the hall.

Then he stopped. What now? He had nowhere to go— no classes, no favorite subject, no purpose. With a shrug, he wandered down to the open common area where students had lunch. He picked an empty table, laid his head on his arms, and tried to zone out.

"Zech?"

He jolted upright, spinning to see who it was. Christie Cunningham stood there, peering through long brown bangs that curled just enough to frame her eyes. For the first time, he noticed she wasn't wearing glasses. Her left eye was a warm, chocolate brown, her right a stormy gray.

"What're *you* doing here?" His question came out more confused than sharp.

"Catching up on schoolwork," Christie said.

"For Johnson?"

"Nope, just some psych stuff through the university."

Zech smirked. "Why am I not surprised?" As he studied her more closely, he noticed faint, purplish bruising on her cheeks. *What's going on there?* he wondered. "So you're not working in the library today?"

"No," Christie said, shaking her head. "There's a whole research class in there. I like it where it's quiet."

"Yeah," he said with a nod. *Why am I even talking to her?*

"So, what're *you* doing out here? Was there more testing in gym today?"

"Lifting, and no." As soon as the word left his mouth, he bit his tongue. *Stupid, stupid, stupid!*

Christie raised an eyebrow. "So what's the deal this time?"

Zech's mind scrambled for an excuse, but came up empty. Finally, he just shrugged and said, "Stuff."

She studied him for so long it felt more like she was drilling boring holes in his face. Finally, she relented with a nod. "So *what are* you doing if you don't have class?"

"Nothing, I guess."

"Gotcha," she said faintly, a little dimple showing in her left cheek. "Everyone needs a break sometimes."

Zech turned away, deciding not to push the conversation further. Christie seemed fine with that, settling into her books. Zech, meanwhile, kept circling back to the same miserable question: *what now?* Everything he wanted, he couldn't do. Everything he could do, he didn't want.

After a long silence, Christie sighed. "Hey, Zech?" Her voice sounded hesitant, almost hopeful.

"Yeah?" he asked dully, turning to her.

She seemed torn, like the words were a battle. At last she said, "If you'd needed help with anything, I'd've given it if you'd asked."

"What?" Zech whirled, banging his shin against the stool's bar. He stared at her. "What are you talking about?"

"You know." Her voice was strained. "If you'd needed help and asked, I'd've done what I could to help you. There's no shame in asking for help with schoolwork."

Zech blinked at her, bewildered. Then suspicion crept in. "Why are you telling me this?" he asked slowly.

"Just thought I'd offer, I guess," she said with a shrug. "I'm always around if someone needs a little help."

His temper flared. "Oh, so you think I'm a basket case?"

"What? No! I just—"

"What, just because I'm out of lifting for a few days, you think I'm floundering? That I'm no good unless I'm slinging weights? Unlike Little Miss Perfect who studies sixteen hours a day and never gets less than an A-plus?"

"No! I'm just saying that if you *did* need help—"

"Well, I *don't* need it, Miss Tutor, and I don't *want* it, so I'm good, thanks."

Christie's eyes widened, hurt flashing across her face. Immediately guilt stabbed at Zech, but before he could say anything, her cheeks flushed with anger.

"Fine!" she snapped, shoving her books into her bag. "If you want to be the reason the class GPA—maybe even the *school's GPA*—drops, that's on you. Good luck with your lifting 'stuff.' I guess that's what you're best at." And with that, she slung her bag over her shoulder and stormed off, leaving Zech with nothing but his thoughts and a silence he now despised.

* * *

"Have a good one!" Mrs. Applegate called from the driver's seat as Zech plodded off the bus.

Zech barely acknowledged her with a nod, then bowed his head and trudged home. At the top of the driveway, he punched in the garage code and stepped inside. Entering the kitchen, a note pinned to the fridge with a round magnet caught his eye. Curious, he pulled it free and read his mother's hurried handwriting.

Zech,

I forgot to tell you before you left this morning, but Mrs. Davis is going to pick you up at home at four o'clock to help me with your punishment. Be good, be humble, and be kind.

Love,
Mom

Immediately his heart sank. *Great. Now she's involved. Just what I need—another person on my back!*

With a sigh, he dropped his backpack by a chair, grabbed a protein bar and a couple cheese sticks, and sat down to wait.

About half an hour later, a car pulled into the drive, and he slipped out through the garage, closing it behind him. A sleek, well-maintained, navy-blue 2020 Ford Vanguard idled there, its paint a little faded but clearly well kept. Feeling awkward, he tapped the passenger window. Mrs. Davis turned with a warm smile and waved him in. Dying inside, he climbed in, setting his bag at his feet.

"Hi, Zech!" she said brightly. "Why the bag?"

Zech shrugged. "Just in case my punishment is being banished to the pits of homework for the next seventy-five years."

She chuckled, though her eyes held a flicker of sadness. "No extra homework today." Her expression shifted to something like excitement. "You know that old bookstore on Main and Plumbdale?"

"The one built, like, forty years ago? Yeah, I *think* so. Mom was freaking out when the city wanted to tear it down. Can't blame them—it's an eyesore."

Either she didn't hear or had elected to ignore that. "My father, Mr. Stroud, bought and developed it years ago. Since the vote, he's been fixing it up for the grand reopening. He could use an extra set of hands."

"Guess I should've worn some old gym clothes if I'm dusting."

Mrs. Davis laughed, warm and amused. "Your outfit's fine. He just needs help putting up the marquee out front, and maybe some odd jobs inside."

"A *marquee?* Kinda fancy for a bookstore."

"You'll see," she said mysteriously. "Now buckle up."

* * *

"Well, here we are!" Mrs. Davis announced as she parked in front of a red-brick building that stood out from the gray offices around it. "That's him."

Zech followed her gaze. A tall man in a black overcoat

was perched on a ladder, adjusting the frame of a canvas archway. His hair was black streaked with gray, but he looked lean and strong.

Mrs. Davis gave two short honks, then opened her door and started toward him. Hesitant, Zech followed. "Got a minute, Dad?" she called. "Or are you doing everything yourself?"

The man laughed, rich and jolly. "I'm fine, Ema. But since you've given me an excuse, I'll play foreman for a while." He climbed down, turning to Zech with a kind, curious smile.

Zech flinched under his gaze. His face was kind, yet solemn, his short graying beard and twinkling blue eyes giving him an air of quiet mystery.

"Zech, this is my father, Michael Gordon Stroud, procurator of Imagine Nation," Mrs. Davis said.

"A pleasure to meet you, young man," Mr. Stroud said, extending a hand. "You can call me Mike. And whom might you be?"

"Zech," he said stiffly, shaking it.

"Zach?"

"Zech. Rhymes with tech. Short for Zechariah."

"Ah, I see!" Mike smiled. "Thanks for bringing him, Ema. I'll call you when we're done. It shouldn't take too long."

"Don't mention it," she said. "It's been a while."

"You and Jonathan are welcome any time, especially now that the vote's over."

Ema smiled. "I love you, Dad!"

"Love you too, Em! See you soon!"

She blew him a kiss and drove off. Zech's heart sank

as she disappeared. *Her name is Ema?! And she acts like . . . a daughter, not a teacher!* The thought both astonished and unsettled him, warming his chest and twisting his gut all at once.

"So," Mike said, turning to him, "you're here to earn money, right?"

Zech raised an eyebrow. "I . . . guess. Just need about twenty-five bucks for a . . . minor home repair."

"Oh? What kind of repair?" Then, seeing Zech tense, he softened. "If you don't mind me asking."

Zech hesitated, then sighed. "I punched a hole in my wall. Long story. I don't wanna talk about it."

Mike's expression grew solemn, but not overtly judgmental—more compassionate than condemning. "Well then," he said, straightening, "we'd better get started. How about you climb up that ladder and check if those beams are locked? The ropes give me trouble sometimes."

Zech waited for mention of pay, but his mother's words echoed: *When you know the right thing to do, don't expect to be rewarded; just do it.*

"Okay," he said, and climbed.

* * *

"Coming along nicely, Zech!" Mike called. "Why don't you come down, grab a drink, and see the the fruits of your labor?"

The only fruit I want is my money! Still, Zech descended. Mike had already set up another ladder so they could work together, but for now he stepped inside and returned with a jug and two cups.

"Homemade apple cider," Mike said, pouring. "Hope you like it!"

"Yeah! I *love* apple cider!" Zech said, surprising himself.

"Then this'll be a treat! Cheers!" He passed Zech a cup, and they tapped their cups together.

Feeling a strange sense of camaraderie with the older man, Zech took a sip—and immediately drained his cup. It was tart, refreshing, perfect. He set his empty cup down and eyed the jug longingly.

"You like it?" Mike asked, amused.

"Love it, actually!"

"Glad to hear it. My Ema's goddaughter, Christie, gave me the recipe!"

Zech froze. "Wait . . . did you say Christie? As in Christie Cunningham?"

"That's right. You know her?"

"Yeah. Yeah, I do." His stomach flipped. Christie Cunningham was Mrs. Davis' goddaughter—and would that make Mike her grandfather? Guilt washed over him for every insult he'd ever thought or thrown at her. *How am I supposed to apologize without sounding like a total idiot?* "Hey, Mr. Stroud—I mean, Mike?" Zech asked quickly, pointing at the marquee. "Why's it shaped like an arch?"

"Ah!" Mike's eyes gleamed. "It's the arch over the entrance to Castle Ilamar, a setting in my newest novel."

"You're an author?"

"Yep! I've written a few stories, but *this* one's special. Come inside, and I'll show you."

"Oh, okay," Zech said awkwardly.

"Something wrong, son?"

"Nothing, sir. It's just . . . I'm not much of a reader. At all. That's more Christie's thing, honestly."

"Oh, that's all right. Tell ya what—this counts as time on the clock."

Zech perked up. *Bribe or not, more time means more pay.* "Okay, let's go."

"Good!" Mike led the way inside.

The lobby was hushed, thick emerald carpets muffling every sound. Rows of tall wooden shelves filled the space like a library, with a wide checkout desk at the front. A carpeted staircase led to the second floor, where Mike guided him down a hall into a cozy office piled with books and papers in tumbled piles on the desk left of the door.

"Aha, here it is!" Mike pulled a paperback from the stack. On its cover was a castle and the title: *The Stone of Ilamar.*

Zech ignored the book, his curiosity tugging at something else. "Mike? I have some other questions for you, if that's okay."

Mike looked a little surprised, but smiled politely. "Go right ahead!"

"Why do you call this place *Imagine Nation?*"

Mike's smile spread wide. "Ah, great question! I once read that just as there's the English nation, or the French nation, we also have the *imagination.* So I thought—why not just call it the Imagine Nation, a place where kids can learn to read, and love it, in a unique and unforgettable way? And the name stuck."

"What do you mean, 'in a unique and unforgettable way'?"

Mike's expression turned thoughtful. "That I can't quite explain. But," he added with a grin and a twinkle in his eye, "I can *show* you."

Zech hesitated. Mike was either being cryptic—or serious. Either way, he was still the boss. *Well,* he thought, *in for a penny, in for a pound.*

"Sure," Zech said. "Show me."

Mike smiled, book in hand, and led him out of the room.

CHAPTER 5

THE DARK ROOM

Zech followed Mike down the hall, his curiosity giving way to apprehension. What exactly did the older man have in store? He wasn't sure Mike meant him any harm, but the man's eagerness and vagueness made his intentions hard to read.

They stopped before a door at the center of the building. Just as Mike reached for the knob, it opened, and a brunette woman with a lined face and kind eyes stepped out, a hardback novel in her hands.

"Oh, hello, Jennifer!" Mike greeted, his smile lighting up his face. "I was just working on the marquee with this young man"—he gestured to Zech—"and was about to show him the Dark Room."

Jennifer smiled, and Zech noticed the silver and gold rings on her left hand. "Don't mind me, dear. I was just leaving. You two enjoy yourselves." Turning to Zech, she added warmly, "It's a pleasure to meet you, young man. You're in for a treat." Then, back to Mike: "There'll be a plate waiting for you, dear."

"I look forward to it, hon."

They kissed lightly, and Jennifer slipped past and disappeared down the hall.

"All right, Zech," Mike said, smiling as he pushed the door closed. Instantly, the room fell into complete darkness.

Zech's stomach tightened, his pulse quickening. "Sir?"

"It's all right," Mike replied calmly. Zech heard the scratch of a match, and soon a dim, golden light flared to life. In its faint glow, Zech saw a lone candlestick on a wooden table in the center of a black-painted, black-carpeted room. Zech watched with curiosity as Mike set the book beside it.

"Come here, Zech. I want to show you how this works."

"How *what* works?" Zech asked warily.

"The power of your imagination."

Zech fought to repress a snort. "What, like a fairy tale?"

Mike only shrugged. "If that's how you imagine it."

"I don't get it," Zech muttered.

"Try this," Mike said, opening the book. "Read the first few lines and visualize them as best you can."

"So, like VR?"

"Yes—except this time, *you* build the world yourself."

That caught Zech off guard. VR usually created everything for him; he hadn't considered building it himself. *Playing pretend was for little kids,* he'd always thought. But now . . .

A VR station in my own head?

Both skeptical and intrigued, he leaned closer and read:

*Stone of emerald, gleaming bright
In the palm of heirling right!
Son or daughter, glowing hotter,
The Stone's light chooseth Ilamar's knight.*

"Poetry?" he asked flatly.

"Keep going," Mike encouraged.

Zech turned the page, relieved to see regular paragraphs:

Once upon a time, in a faraway land, there lived a sorrowful king over a sorrowful realm. Ever since the kingdom was founded, the House of Ilamar had ruled—generation after generation inheriting the throne, though not always the eldest child.

Long ago, when the family was still a clan, a seer gifted them a mysterious green gem. Upon their rise to the throne, Lady Esmeralda prophesied that any descendant who held the glowing Stone would rule Ilamar by right.

So it had been for centuries. But in this unhappy time, the Stone was stolen, as well as the newborn prince, and neither were ever recovered. And so the land wept. Yet Queen Esperanza clung to hope. Though her son was presumed lost with the Stone," she trusted the prophecy, believing he might one day return, claim the Stone, and fulfill his destiny.

As he read, the darkness around him shifted. He caught flashes—snippets of scenes matching the words: a king weeping on his throne; a green gem held aloft; a woman praying at a bedside; a bawling baby boy being snatched away; the echo of a battle cry. Startled, Zech looked up.

"What was that?" he blurted.

Mike's expression was unreadable. "What was what?"

"That noise, those people, the Stone! Where did it come from? How'd you do that?"

"Me?" Mike smiled. "Oh, *I* didn't do anything."

Zech was absolutely baffled. Reflexively, he checked his watch. Six o'clock. "Sorry, sir, but I should probably go. Mom'll be worried about me."

Mike blinked. "Mercy, you're right!" he cried. "Sorry, Zech. I didn't mean to keep you so long. I'll call Ema to pick you up. Oh—here." He dug into his pocket and handed Zech a ten-dollar bill. "For your help today. Thank you, son." He blew out the candle, and together they left the room.

* * *

That night, Zech tossed and turned, his mind stuck between Christie and the Dark Room.

How do I apologize to her?

Was that magic?

Should I write a note? Or just say it in person?

But if Mike didn't cause those visions . . . who did?

With a frustrated groan, he punched his mattress. Nothing made sense. He'd tried drafting an apology to read off to Christie, but each attempt turned into a dead end before he erased it. Eventually, he wrote down some bullet points, then flopped down with a weary sigh. For the first time in a long while, he whispered a prayer that wasn't purely selfish desperation: *God, I need Your help; I'm totally lost.*

Then, like a lightning bolt, a thought hit him: Christie. She was Mike's god-granddaughter. She'd been inside Imagine

Nation before—*and* she loved reading! Maybe *she* already knew what that room was. Maybe *she* could explain it. Excited but exhausted, Zech jotted down a note on his watch, then dropped it onto the nightstand. Despite his racing thoughts, sleep claimed him quickly, pulling him into dreams filled with battle cries and hidden treasures.

CHAPTER 6

THE DAUGHTER OF THE KING

Zech did his best to keep a low profile in English class. Mrs. Davis had asked him about his time at Imagine Nation on the way home, and he'd tried to be polite but brief. He prayed she wouldn't bring it up again. All that morning, he still couldn't think of the right time—or the right way—to talk to Christie. Since he no longer had lifting, he decided to retreat to the commons after class and mull it over some more. Still, the clock hands moved slowly.

Finally, after what felt like an eternity, the bell rang. Zech gathered his things quickly, melted into the crowd, ducked into the bathroom until it thinned, and then slipped out toward the commons. At a table, hunched over his watch, he scrolled through the outline that he'd written for himself, ending with a bold reminder: "ASK CHRISTIE ABOUT MIKE'S ROOM!!!"

But how do I ask her without sounding crazy—especially when I'm not sure I'm not crazy?!

"Zech?"

He jumped. His greatest hope and worst fear stood

before him: Christie Cunningham, a thick book in hand, her expression equal parts confused and resigned.

Taking a deep breath, he forced out a greeting. "Hey." The courage drained from him the moment the word left his lips.

"You're here a lot," Christie said with a slight frown. "What's up with lifting *this* time?"

Still reeling from yesterday, and staring into her beautiful, mismatched eyes, Zech couldn't lie. "I dunno," he admitted. "I'm not in there anymore."

Her eyes widened, then narrowed. "Really? What happened?"

"I . . . um . . ." *Blast it! Why can't you just spit it out?!* But he knew why: his pride held him back. "Look," he said, lowering his voice. "Remember how I said I didn't need help with anything?"

"Sure," Christie said, nodding slowly.

"Well, that wasn't exactly true. And I'm sorry for what I said yesterday."

"Oh." Christie looked taken aback at first, but then she smiled hesitantly. "That's all right. I should apologize too. What I said about your GPA and lifting was totally uncalled-for. I'm sorry."

Now it was Zech's turn to be taken aback. Maybe she had meant those things yesterday, but he brushed it aside. *Be the bigger person.* "Yeah, me too. Totally uncalled-for."

"I forgive you," Christie said softly. "I just meant I understand not wanting help, wanting to do it all yourself.

But sometimes that's not realistic. *I need a little help some-times too.*"

"Wait, *you?!* The super-nerd?" The words slipped out, and immediately he kicked himself.

"Sure!" she said, setting her book on the table. "My eyes aren't that good, so I sometimes need a little extra time with my work. That's why I sit in the back—study halls run late, and by the time I get there, all but the back row is taken."

"Oh!" Guilt swelled in him. No wonder she hated distractions. "I'm sorry. I hadn't thought of that."

"Don't be," Christie said lightly. "That's just life for me."

Suddenly he remembered his note, and his stomach knotted. "Hey, uh, Christie?"

"Yeah?" She sat down beside him, giving him a curious look.

How do I say this? "Um . . . you know Mike Stroud, right?" *Stupid question!*

Her eyes lit up. "Sure! He's Mrs. Davis' father, and I *love* his bookstore!"

"Right. Well, um . . ." Zech hesitated. "I was over there yesterday helping him set up—you make great apple cider, by the way—"

"Thank you," Christie said with a giggle, her cheeks flushing slightly.

"Yeah, it was amazing. Anyway, he invited me up to see this book he was working on, took me to this dark room, had me read—it was pitch black, aside from a candle—and then . . ."

To his shock, Christie nodded, a knowing smile on her lips. "You imagined what was in the book, and it came to life, didn't it?"

"It was like I was there—or it was there with me! He said it wasn't some special effect, but—wait, you *knew*?!"

"Of course! Mr. Stroud showed me that room when I was in fourth grade; it helped me fall in love with reading. I'm glad he showed *you* too. It's *so* worth experiencing." With that, she opened her book.

Zech felt like that was all he was going to get out of her. "Well, thanks for talking, Christie," he said, starting to leave.

"Wait, Zech?"

He stopped, halfway turned, backpack on his shoulder. "Yeah?"

"What I said about helping you with schoolwork still stands."

He stared, stunned, then shrugged. "Yeah, sure. Maybe."

"Great!" She tore a scrap of paper from a pad, scribbled on it, and handed it to him. "If you ever want a study session, you can reach me here."

"Cool. Thanks." He slipped the number into his pocket and walked away, new questions pressing in on him.

* * *

These new questions were still buzzing through his mind when he reached his bus stop. *Christie had been in the Dark Room, but did she know how the Dark Room worked? Why was she still willing to do a study session with him? And why had he accepted?*

Yet answers eluded him. When the bus pulled up, he waved to Mrs. Applegate, then hopped off. Just as he turned toward home, a thump and startled cry stopped him cold.

Christie Cunningham stood a few yards away, her book bag askew. Facing her was Trace Seamore, bully king of Odessa High. Quickly Zech ducked behind a hedge, heart pounding.

"Well, well, well," Trace said, his voice smug and cold. "If it isn't the prettiest thing in Odessa High."

"What do you want, Trace?" Christie's voice was weary.

Trace smirked, his teeth glinting in the sun like a shark's. "What? A guy can't check on a lady he's missed?"

"You mean since yesterday?" she asked dryly.

Anger flickered in his sky-blue eyes, then faded. "So, whatcha up to these days?"

Christie stayed silent.

Suddenly, he backhanded her across the right cheek. Her glasses slid down her nose. "I ask you a question, you answer. Got it?"

Zech's anger flared, but he stayed hidden. Trace was two hundred pounds, and built like Hercules, and rumor had it that he was a black belt in karate. Wrestling season in their tiny school district hardly compared. And while Zech figured he was physically stronger than Trace, he wasn't about to test his luck.

"Please, just let me go home," Christie said. "I don't have money, and I'm not interested in you."

Trace's face darkened. "Oh, I see. Think you're too good for me, huh?" He slapped her again, hard. Her glasses flew off, one lens skittering to the pavement. With a sneer, he crushed it under his heel. "You still owe me lunch tomorrow." With that, he turned away, running his fingers through his dirty-blond curls.

Christie winced, holding her cheek. Zech's instincts screamed attack, but Trace was already gone. He cursed himself—he should've stepped in sooner. *How could you just let that happen?!*

Christie bent to retrieve her bent glasses, now with only one lens. Zech thought he saw a pearly tear slide from her exposed left eye. Then she pulled her hood up and walked toward home. Guilt heavy in his chest, Zech turned away and trudged toward his own house.

CHAPTER 7

THE GEM IN THE DARK

"Well, Zech, I think that looks great for today," Mike Stroud said from the bottom of the ladder. "This'll look sharp for the grand reopening tomorrow. And from what I hear, you've got yourself a three-day weekend out of it!"

"Wait—what?" Zech asked, coming down the ladder and staring at his employer in astonishment.

"So Ema tells me. She convinced the city council to allow a one-time village holiday so everyone can come at nine o'clock." He chuckled. "Guess she's really been givin' 'em the business for trying to shut Imagine Nation down, huh?"

Zech snorted. "Yeah—guess so." *Ironic,* he thought. *Mrs. Davis fighting for a day off school? Now I've heard everything!* But then he started thinking about the book in that strange room, and frustration crept back in. "Hey, Mr. Stroud?" he asked, trying to mask it.

"Yes?" Mike asked.

"Well, I've been thinking," Zech said carefully, "and I really don't get that book or that room you showed me on Monday."

"Oh?" Mike looked at him quizzically.

Zech nodded. "I just don't understand how it works. If it isn't *you,* then what *is* it? Is it the book, or the room, or anything at all? Or is it all just in my head?"

Mike beamed, letting out one of his rich, grandfatherly laughs. "Of *course* it's all in your head—or at least *half* of it is. The other half is on the page."

Zech frowned. "I don't get it."

Mike laughed again, shorter this time, then grew thoughtful, though his eyes still twinkled. "Imagination is something you find within yourself. But like anything in your mind, it's shaped by what you put *into* it. The room just shuts out distractions so you can focus on the words and imagine what they might be like if you were there."

Zech blinked slowly. Now he understood why Mike had likened it to a VR set in your head—except *you* got to create the world instead of a machine. "Can I—do you—could I try it again?"

Mike's face lit up like Christmaskah had come early. "I was hoping you'd ask. Come on!"

* * *

Caleb was running for his life. His breath came in sharp gasps, lungs burning, heart pounding in his ears as his feet slapped the flagstones in a frantic rhythm.

"*Rashta!*"—Scoundrel!—the butcher roared after him.

As if answering the curse, the man's hounds bayed not ten yards away, closing fast. Caleb pushed harder, cursing his luck. Why had the old man set his dogs on him? He hadn't even stolen anything—yet. At this point, his reputation as a thief and beggar (which, to be fair, he was) was so sealed that if he ever tried to hire himself out, they'd immediately turn him over to the garrison.

Starving on the streets or starving in jail, he thought, as he always had—though this time with less bravado. *At least here I can run free.*

But even that was slipping away. The hounds were closing in. Without thinking, Caleb darted left out of the alley and onto the main road, sprinting for the city gates. He squeezed through just as the guards looked up in surprise. A heartbeat later, the gates clanged shut. Not daring to stop, Caleb kept running until he'd gone nearly a mile into the pine forest west of the city. *Well, guess I'm sleeping outside the city tonight,* he thought—and was about to mutter it aloud when suddenly his foot caught. He pitched forward, bracing for pain.

But the impact came later than expected. He landed on something soft, though his elbows and knees smarted against the ground beneath. Dazed, he felt around and discovered pine needles on the stone floor of a hole about six feet across. Darkness pressed in.

"Well," he muttered, "guess if I've gotta fall into a cave, at least it's a cushioned one. Shame I can't tarp the top, or I'll be rained out. Hopefully I can climb out in the morning—if Fortune favors."

With that, he started digging through the pine needles to make a rough bed—when something bright caught his eye. Squinting, he saw a faint green glow near his right hand.

Fingers brushing something cold and hard, he grabbed it and held it up. A small, green gem—round like a pearl—lay in his palm, gleaming brighter by the second on own.

* * *

Zech gasped, shielding his eyes. But when he did, the print vanished, and his awareness returned.

"That was . . . so real!" he said, astonished.

Mike smiled. "Looks like you're getting the hang of it."

"I literally *was him!*" Zech said, still shaken. "My heart was racing; my gut lurched when he fell—I can still see the gem glowing in my—his—hand!" He looked at Mike in the dim candlelight. "Does this work with any book?"

"Sure, as long as you can imagine it—though not all things are always worth imagining."

Zech thought of some of the books he'd had to slog through in middle school and figured he understood. Then a thought surfaced—one he tried to shove away but couldn't.

"Everything all right, Zech?" Mike asked gently. "You look . . . unsettled."

"Sorry, sir, it's nothing," Zech said quickly. "It's just . . ."

"It's all right, son. Whatever it is, you can tell me."

Zech fought with himself, then blurted, "Could I borrow your book?" His cheeks flushed. "Please?"

Mike laughed softly. "Tell you what. I'll let you come by every Monday and Thursday after school, just like this week, and read here for an hour—but only if you promise to do your homework first. And that includes the nights you're not here," he added with a stern look.

Zech's eyes widened. "How did you—" Then he remembered his mother's note about Mrs. Davis. "She told you, didn't she?" he asked miserably.

"Everything *she* knows," Mike said with a shrug. "I don't know what your mother shared, and that's none of my business. But she and your mom go way back. I'm just trying to do my part to help. I suggest *you* do the same."

The fifth commandment—"Honor your father and mother"—flashed through Zech's mind. He bristled at the thought of his deadbeat father, then winced at the image of his exhausted mother. And then, unexpectedly, he thought of Christie's kind, earnest face and her offer of help.

"So, do we have a deal?" Mike asked, holding out a hand.

"Yes, sir," Zech said—surprising himself with the conviction in his voice—and shook it.

"Good!" Mike said, pulling him in close and clapping him on the back.

Three hours later, Zech set down his pen, feeling more drained than he had in ages. For once, he'd answered every question—even when he didn't know the answer. Maybe some would be right. Maybe the effort would count. More than once, he'd wanted to quit, but each time he'd thought of his deal, Christie's face, and an old saying his parents had agreed on: *Once you put your hand to something, you'd better do all you can to finish it.*

Well, at least I can sleep in a little, he thought. *And maybe*

Christie will be at the opening tomorrow—though I'm not sure I deserve to talk to her. He hadn't seen her since the bus stop incident two days ago, and part of him feared he might not again.

As he packed up, his eyes fell on the red Sharpie he'd stolen. Slowly, he uncapped it, staring at the point. He had promised Mike he'd do his homework. But would someone who made that promise also steal a teacher's marker—or use it the way he had? Would that guy defend the girl he liked, or hide in fear? And of the two, which one was real, and which was just pretending? Deep down, he feared he already knew.

CHAPTER 8

NEW BEGINNINGS

Michael Stroud rose from his knees and opened his eyes. Standing beside his bed, he stretched his weary body and yawned. He'd been up since six o'clock that morning, preparing for the big day. A large part of that preparation had been prayer, asking God's will to be done through the event. But even more pressing on his heart was Zechariah Forshaw and the countless prayers he'd lifted for him.

Most would find it strange how much he'd come to care for the boy since Ema first told him about the situation. Over the years, as Imagine Nation had welcomed countless young souls, Michael's empathy had deepened. Though he was only pushing sixty, he'd come to see a pattern in people: the same eyes, the same pain, the same longing, appearing again and again in different faces. In them he had seen spirit, loneliness, rebellion, heartache, regret—sometimes with a change of heart and sometimes not. He sighed, remembering some of the hardest cases he'd witnessed.

"O Lord God, please help this young man," he whispered, turning toward the door.

Just then, a knock sounded. "You ready, honey?" Jennifer's sweet voice floated through the wood like a soft hymn.

"Yes, dear," he said, walking to the door. Ema and Jonathan, his daughter and son-in-law, followed closely behind Jennifer.

"So, how's Zech doing?" Ema asked as they walked down the hall toward the stairs from the flat to the store below.

"Oh, wonderful!" Mike said. "He's been a great help getting everything ready, now that I'm so old." His smirk aimed at his daughter carried a playful irony.

"You *need* it, Dad," Ema said sternly. "You aren't as young as you used to be."

"I know, I know," Mike replied, holding up a hand. "I like to do what I can on my own—but I *do* appreciate Zech's help, truly."

"Well, *I* think it all turned out for the best," Jennifer said warmly.

"So far," Jonathan added. "It hasn't started yet. But I'm sure it will."

* * *

"I'll admit, Zech, I don't understand *why* you want to go, but *this* is exactly the kind of event I'd *want* you to attend—grounded or not."

Zech winced, emotions churning like a cauldron, yet he shrugged. "Mr. Stroud expects me there," he admitted, then added in almost a whisper, "and I figure it's the right thing to do."

His mother studied him a long moment, and Zech felt the urge to squirm under her gaze. But then she shrugged. "Well, grab a bagel." To him, this meant: "Hurry up and grab something quick; I don't have time to make you anything else." By eight-thirty, the Forshaws were climbing into Corban's old Toyota on a crisp October morning.

At the store, Zech found himself amidst a bustling crowd, a blue ribbon stretched across the entrance. The mayor spoke of community and growth—words Zech neither understood nor cared about. His eyes searched desperately for Christie, but the crowd was thick. Then Michael Stroud stepped up to the podium, and Zech's attention fixed instantly.

"Good morning, all!" Michael's voice carried cheerily. Many returned his greeting, mostly adults of his daughter's age or older. "I'm humbled and honored to be here today and want to thank the city council for giving everyone an extra day off to join us. Thanks to my daughter, Ema Davis, for helping make it happen"—he shot her a knowing, mischievous wink—"and most importantly, my God and Savior, Jesus Christ, for bringing everything together."

Applause.

"As some of you know, I inherited this shop from my father after he tragically died of leukemia. I had dreams of grad school, of changing the world, but three things convinced me to stay: my father's love for the people who came here, the education and guidance he gave me, and the prayers of my pastor and the woman who would become my wife."

He paused, letting the words sink in. "By God's grace, I

realized I could change the world right here in my hometown. Imagine Nation is more than a bookstore—it's a library, a place to learn, connect, and be inspired. In this age of loneliness, I'm honored to provide a place of joy, wonder, and imagination. And if you can't find what you seek *here,* ask Reverend Presley at Our Lord's Chapel—or my son-in-law, Jonathan."

Laughter and applause followed, a loud "Amen!" echoing from somewhere in the crowd.

With a gracious smile, Mike accepted a pair of scissors from the mayor. "Once again, thank you all for being here! Behind this ribbon is a marquee designed to resemble the entrance to Castle Ilamar, a setting in my latest novel, *The Stone of Ilamar,* available inside—and yes, I do autographs." He smiled playfully. "Step inside and allow yourself to expect anything— even what you least expect. Because here, just like the space between your ears, anything is possible. Welcome, one and all, to Imagine Nation!"

He raised the scissors and cut the ribbon. A gust of wind lifted the ends, forming a smaller arch before dropping as the crowd surged forward, controlled only by the sheriff's deputies. Dazed, Zech wandered among the familiar surroundings, like a sparrow seeking rest. Nothing caught his interest—until a thick, leather-bound tome drew his eyes:

THE HOLY BIBLE
LEGACY STANDARD BIBLE

Zech felt inexplicably drawn. Growing up, he'd known the Jewish Tanakh at home and only glimpsed the New

Covenant at Mrs. Davis' house. *This* was something new—a complete Bible of his *own!* He carried it toward the checkout, where Mike was busy ringing up books, chatting with customers, and autographing copies of *The Stone of Ilamar.*

Then Zech saw her—Christie Cunningham, without her glasses, accompanied by a woman who must have been her mother. She held another copy of Mike's book. Zech approached, straining to hear over the noise.

"Hello, Mrs. Cunningham! Christie!" Mike greeted. "I take it you found the large print section okay?"

"Yes, thank you," Christie said, a little sheepish. "No one else was around except some nice ladies browsing who said hi."

"Well, wonderful," Mike said, taking her book. "You want me to sign this for you?"

"Yes, thank you!" Christie said, though Zech thought he caught a tired, apprehensive look in her mother's eyes.

Mike smiled warmly. "I'll sign it nice and big for you."

"You and I *both* know that no one can read your signature *anyway!*" Christie joked.

"Well, *I* can!" Mike protested, eyes twinkling with amusement.

Christie indicated her mother. "She says it looks like my dad's, and *he's* a doctor!"

Mike laughed again, handing the book back. "Stop by anytime—you're welcome in the Dark Room or for homework help."

Christie smiled. "I will, thank you!"

Zech stood frozen as he watched the Cunninghams leave. *She needs large print?!* That explained so much—why she always seemed busy, why she only acknowledged him up close. *Is she . . . visually impaired?*

Feeling numb and detached from himself, he walked up and placed his Bible on the counter. Mike looked at him, then nodded knowingly.

"She'll tell you in her own time."

Zech felt guilty, yet relieved. "How much do I owe you?" he asked, his voice sounding dead in his own ears.

Mike shook his head. "Nothing."

"But—"

Mike held up a hand. "Save it for your home repair. This book's the greatest gift you can give anyone. Take it."

Zech hesitated, then nodded. "Okay. But I *will* pay you back one day."

"No need," Mike said, handing it over. "It's a gift."

* * *

That evening, after synagogue, Zechariah Forshaw sat in his room with his new Bible, wrestling with his thoughts. The service had been on Leviticus 16, *Yom Kippur*, and the Messiah's death and resurrection. Isaiah 52:13–53:12 tore at him, especially 53:4–6:

> *Surely our griefs He Himself bore,*
> *And our sorrows He carried,*
> *Yet we ourselves esteemed Him stricken,*
> *Smitten of God, and afflicted.*

But He was pierced through for our transgressions,
He was crushed for our iniquities;
The chastening for our peace fell upon Him,
And by His wounds we are healed.
All of us like sheep have gone astray,
Each of us has turned to his own way;
But Yahweh has caused the iniquity of us all to fall on Him.

He traced his eyes down the Ten Commandments on the plaque over his bed, recalling the day his parents had brought it home from a summer trip to the Holy Land when Zech was small. "Keeping these," his father had said, standing him before the plaque after he'd nailed them into the wall, "is how we honor *Hashem.*" Now all he saw was a list of all his shortcomings glaring back at him—and he hated how much he'd loved those sins. And then, as if he wasn't feeling enough torment, Yeshua's Sermon on the Mount started coming back to him: anger as murder, lust as adultery, and covetousness as idolatry, according to Saul of Tarsus.

"What do I do?" he whispered, then cried out in anguish: "God, *what do I do now?!*"

Nothing came.

Sighing, he opened to John 19 again, imagining the suffering, the agony, the triumph, and the resurrection. Chapter 20:30–31 echoed in his mind: "Therefore many other signs Jesus also did in the presence of the disciples, which are not written in this book; but these things have been written so that you may believe that Jesus is the Christ, the Son of God, and that believing you may have life in His name."

"For God so loved the world, that He gave His only begotten Son, that whoever believes in Him shall not perish, but have eternal life" (John 3:16). The words finally made sense. Then he remembered Rabbi Jonathan Davis' words: "If you confess with your mouth Jesus as Lord, and believe in your heart that God raised Him from the dead, you will be saved" (Romans 10:9).

Tears, wonder, grief, and joy flooded him, and all he could manage was: "*Adonai*—Yeshua—I believe in You. I'm so sorry." Despite his sparse words, he meant exactly what the verses said. But somehow, he perceived that it was enough.

Opening his eyes, he found, to his surprise, that his room looked different—foreign, yet shamefully familiar. And the more he looked at the posters, the more he hated them. Dark, lewd, and grotesque, they seemed now. In a rush, he tore them down, leaving only the Ten Commandments. Standing amidst the mess, he felt a spark of determination ignite in his heart.

"Lord, I'm gonna need Your help again. I've got a lot of work to do."

CHAPTER 9

THE PASTORAL PRINCESS

Coming to the end of the street, Caleb ducked behind a mound of rubbish as another gaggle of clerical maidens passed by. Their pristine white dresses and shawls looked absurdly out of place against the grimy streets of Sarna. He knew they were only trying to help the poor, but he didn't want pity—or charity. He preferred to be—as he called it—self-reliant. Still, they *had* given him breakfast.

Soon their footsteps faded. Caleb let out a sigh of relief. Grabbing the melon, he split it open on the ground and began to feast. He hadn't eaten since late morning the previous day. The fruit was juicy, almost as sweet as honey, such as the delicacies that he fancied only the royal family and their nobles ever tasted. When he finished, he tossed the broken rind onto the rubbish heap and considered venturing out—but then froze.

A strange, lilting song floated toward him, hauntingly beautiful. Cautiously, he crept toward the sound. It was both triumphant and oddly sad, though he couldn't make out all of the words. It reminded him of the hymns sung by the Holy Order of Pascha—which included the very sisters he had just avoided. The voice was strong and vibrant, gliding up and down the melody with a smooth, steady tone.

Caleb edged closer and froze again, this time in awe. In the center of the town square stood a girl his age, singing with abandon, her face soft, round, and beautiful, her hair and eyes covered by a handwoven scarlet veil. Her skin was sun-kissed, a shade or two darker than his sun-kissed complexion—reminiscent of the traders from Jehellem.

"Peace to you, friend!" she called.

Caleb jumped, startled. "And to you," he stammered, suddenly tongue-tied.

The girl's warm smile remained. "I am Sister Charis, maidservant of the Anointed Lord," she said. "And whom might you be?"

Caleb struggled for words. Finally, he muttered, "I'm no one."

"That is more than I know," Sister Charis said. "But surely God knows best."

Caleb chuffed. "If you say so."

Charis regarded him for a moment, then asked, "Do you believe in the Anointed Lord?"

"I believe in Fortune."

"Perhaps you see only the back of the coin, while *I* behold the King's face."

Caleb frowned, confused, fidgeting with the small green gem still in his pocket. Slowly, her words began to click. What *he* saw as Fortune, *she* saw as God at work. "Yeah," he said slowly, initially more to himself than to her, then said more conversationally, "Yeah, I guess that could be true."

Charis beamed. "Do you understand the words in the song I just sang?"

Caleb initially wanted to say no—but as he brought his fist close, squinting at the green light shining through his fingers, the words he *had* heard as he'd drawn closer began to echo in his mind:

Oh, blessed be the Anointed King,
A ransom hanging on a tree!
He took away Death's cruel sting,
And rose to grant life to them that believe.

"Yeah, it sounds familiar," he admitted, surprised. "But what does it mean?"

Charis opened her mouth, but suddenly screamed as another street urchin grabbed her by the shoulder and pulled her to the ground, raising her veil triumphantly in his free right hand.

White-hot fury surged through Caleb, and he darted forward, fists clenched. "Leave her alone!" he shouted, feeling stupid and desperate.

To his amazement, the boy froze, eyes fixed first on Caleb's hand, then his face, before turning tail and fleeing like a deer from the hunter. Caleb stared after him, then remembered Charis. "You all right?"

Charis didn't answer at first, eyes closed as though elsewhere. "Sister Charis? Are you all right?"

"Oh!" She sat up, dazed. "Yes, I am well . . . I must again ask your pardon—I never asked you for your name."

"That's fine. I'm Caleb."

"Caleb!" Her eyes widened, though they focused on nothing. Then she straightened and put on her veil. "Thank you, Caleb. I owe you my life. But you must trust me now."

"Trust you . . . how? You're not going to turn me over to the garrison, are you?"

"No. But you *must* come with me—to the elders of our order, or as close to them as God allows."

"But why?"

"The One who died for you, the One in the song, granted me a vision about you."

"Me?" Caleb's jaw dropped.

"I promise I'll explain everything soon. Please, Caleb— even if you don't trust me, trust *Him!*"

Caleb shook his head. "You don't understand. I'm not holy—I'm just a petty street urchin—*rashta*, they call me, and—"

"He *died* for the *rashtat*," she said. Caleb marveled that she not only knew the term, but used it. "Won't you forsake that way and cling to the One who loves you?"

* * *

Zech slammed the book shut, looking at Mike. "Sir, are you some kind of prophet?"

Mike's eyes widened, amused. "No, not that I know of. Why?"

"Because it feels like you wrote this book specifically for *me*, even before we'd met!"

Mike laughed. "Some say the best stories let us see a bit of ourselves—even if we don't like it."

"No! I mean—sorry if I sounded rude! It's just relatable," Zech said, embarrassed.

Mike nodded, handing him another ten. "Thanks for helping put things away, Zech. I've really appreciated your help over the last week." He paused. Zech didn't move. "Is something wrong?"

Zech bit his lip, then said, "Sir, last weekend, I . . . gave my life to Yeshua."

Mike's eyes lit up. "Praise the Lord!"

Zech continued. "But about this home repair—I want to fix or replace *all* the drywall in my room. Could I please work here to raise the money for that?"

Mike paused, genuinely surprised. "Does your mother know?"

"No—I wanted it to be a surprise."

Mike eyed him searchingly for a long moment, then asked, "Is there any part of you that wants to do this to alleviate your own feelings of guilt and shame?"

Zech nodded slightly, then quickly added, "But it would make *her* happy too! 'Honor your father and mother,' right?"

Mike studied him a bit longer, then smiled. "All right, son. Just ask your mom first. But if she says yes, you can work part-time and still do homework. I could use the help anyway."

"Yes, sir!" Zech said.

Mike's grin widened. "Looks like I'll need to give you a raise."

* * *

Walking through the commons, lunch in hand, Zech felt lighter than he had in ages. It felt like fresh air to his stifled soul. *If this was what atonement felt like,* he thought, *he could get used to it.*

His thoughts darkened, however, as they drifted to Christie. Where *was* she? Was she okay? Was she ever coming back? He prayed that she was getting everything she needed, whatever that was.

Just then, Zech spotted her—no glasses, sack lunch in hand, and completely oblivious to Trace Seamore barreling toward her with his usual posse of goons and gagglers behind him. Immediately, panic seized Zech, and he tried waving to Christie, but to no avail. *What should he do?* Then Zech's eyes jumped to his watch. He opened the video app and hit record, unseen.

Trace Seamore sped up, sidling up to Christie. Zech saw her body language react to the bully when he was mere feet away—far too late. Trace shoved Christie and snatched her sack lunch, holding it up like a trophy. "Oops!" he said mockingly. "Didn't see ya there." His posse snickered.

Christie sighed, looking more resigned and irritated than anything else. "Why?" she asked.

"You still owe me from last week," Trace said menacingly.

"Please give it back, Trace," Christie said, resigned. "I didn't pay for that one, my *mom* did. If you want lunch, come with me and I'll buy *you one.*"

Once again, he saw rage kindling in Trace's eyes. But Zech knew he couldn't stand idly by this time, so he darted forward, stopping between Trace and Christie. "Everything okay here?"

Trace glared. "Who are you?"

"Zechariah Forshaw, at your service. That offer of buying you lunch sounds pretty fair to *me,*" Zech said, trying to stall for as long as he could while he thought of a plan.

Trace's icy gaze traced Zech up and down, sizing him up. "Forshaw," he mouthed, as if trying to remember something. Then his lips drew down into a snarl. "You're part of one of the Jewish families around here, aren't you?"

Zech shrugged. "So what if I am?"

"Because," Trace growled, "I don't like you and your ilk."

Just then, Zech saw Mrs. Davis enter the commons. Frantically, he tried to catch her eye—and succeeded! "Really," he said loudly. "Because *I'm* not a big fan of people who hit girls or steal their lunches and don't know when to back off when she clearly doesn't—"

Before Zech knew what had happened, he found himself blinking up at the ceiling, head throbbing, lunch gone, wondering how he'd gotten there. Then he saw Trace's fist aimed straight at Christie's right eye.

"Gavin Trace Seamore!" Time froze as Mrs. Davis intervened. Trace's fist halted inches from Christie's face.

"What in all creation happened here?" Mrs. Davis barked.

Trace's mouth worked silently; then he mumbled, "He started it."

"Are you sure? Because to *me,* and anyone *else* watching, it *looked* like you were about to punch out a fellow student—and *my goddaughter.*"

Dead silence.

Just then, a man with short, graying black hair wearing a blue uniform emerged from one of the hallways. He took in the scene like he was studying a chessboard. Finally, he turned to Mrs. Davis. "Problem, ma'am?" he asked, his voice low and powerful, like a panther prepared to pounce.

"Deputy Gaines," Mrs. Davis said with a satisfied smile. "Please take this young man to the principal's office while I check on Christie and Zech. And call the nurse too."

"Yes, ma'am," the resource officer said, then took Trace by the arm and led him away.

Immediately Mrs. Davis' ire cooled as she checked on the children. "Are you all right, honey?" she asked Christie.

"Yeah, just a little shaken," Christie said, her legs shaking slightly as Mrs. Davis helped her up.

Her godmother frowned dubiously, but nodded, then turned to Zech. "Are you okay, Zech?"

"Yeah, just banged my head," Zech admitted, stopping the video and pushing himself up with his hands. "I dunno *what* he hit me with, but it probably looks sick as all get-out on my watch."

"Wait, on your watch? You mean you were *recording* all this?" Mrs. Davis looked hopeful, even excited.

Zech hesitated, remembering stories he'd heard about unauthorized recordings getting people into trouble. But then he rallied and said, "Yeah. Thought if nothing else, it'd make for a good backup plan."

Mrs. Davis furrowed her brow for a moment. "Zech, I need you to come with us to the principal's office—with your watch. Then I'll take you to see the nurse."

Zech nodded, and soon he and Christie were following Mrs. Davis down the hall, neither saying anything, the uncertainty mounting. Eventually, they reached the principal's office, where Deputy Gaines stood guard at the door. Mrs. Jenkins, a plump woman with bleached blonde hair who looked older than she was, sat behind her large desk with a vapid expression on her face. Across the desk from her sat Trace, cool as a cucumber.

"Well, Mrs. Davis," Mrs. Jenkins said with her usual airy condescension. "From what he tells me, Mr. Forshaw accosted Mr. Seamore in the hallway after the latter narrowly avoided a collision with Miss Cunningham and was merely acting in self-defense against a fellow student who misunderstood the situation and attacked him. What say you?"

Ema Davis smiled and calmly guided the truth: Trace had attacked. She nodded then explained how she had stepped out of her classroom to stretch her legs, saw the confrontation, and intervened. When Mrs. Jenkins asked for proof, Mrs. Davis smiled, and Zech got the impression that she'd been waiting for this for a long time. "I'm glad you asked, Mrs. Jenkins. Zech, would you mind?"

* * *

"I still can't believe that actually *worked!*" Zech said to Christie as they left the bus stop and began the short walk to her house. "Suspended through Thanksgiving break? That's hardcore for her!"

Christie laughed. "I think the look on Trace's face said it all. Between the video and Miss Ema's—I mean, Mrs. Davis'—testimony, he *knew* he was cooked." Then she flushed a little and averted her eyes. "Thanks for escorting me home. I really appreciate it."

"No prob!" Zech said. "I just want you to be safe. I didn't want to see you get hurt again." Immediately, he kicked himself.

Christie looked like she was about to ask something, then realized what he'd just said. "Oh," she said.

Now it was Zech's turn to flush and avert his gaze. "*I* should be the one apologizing—for—yeah, sorry for not doing something the *first* time," he said. "Then you wouldn't've gotten hurt, and your glasses might still be intact."

To Zech's relief, Christie smiled. "I forgive you. Besides, I can get my glasses replaced. Thankfully, he only broke the lens over my *good* eye, so I can actually read okay."

Zech nodded. "Well, *that's* good."

"But why *did* you intervene? What changed between today and last week?"

Zech's stomach lurched. *How was he to* answer? At length, he said, "God tells us in the *Tanakh*—you know, the Hebrew Bible—to defend the rights of the oppressed and to love your neighbor as yourself. And Yeshua tells us to do the same."

Christie stared at him. "You've changed, Zech!"

He blinked. "You really think so?"

"You're not the same cocky slacker I knew a week ago." Then she blushed. "No offense."

"Oh, none taken! I *was* a real *narish*, I know!"

"Narish?"

"A jerk."

"Oh." Her face turned pensive. "Well, if Jesus has something to do with it—well, that would certainly explain it." She paused, and when Zech didn't reply, she continued. "Trust in Jesus changes everything," she said.

Zech nodded. "I guess I didn't realize just how much trusting in Him would change my life."

"Oh yes! It changes everything! Well, here we are."

Just then, they arrived at her cheery yellow house on a quiet street, an apple tree growing in the front yard. Zech whistled. "Your place is awesome! Is that where you get your apple cider?"

"Yeah," Christie said with a modest smile. "Here, pick one!"

So Zech plucked a plump red one as he passed and bit into it. It was crisp, tart, and utterly refreshing—just like her cider. Christie smiled at his expression, then gestured for him to follow her. She led the way up the porch steps and through the front door into a large foyer. There, eyes red with worry, stood Mrs. Cunningham.

"Christie!" she cried, stepping out and enveloping her daughter in the tightest hug Zech had ever seen. "Oh, my sweet baby! Mrs. Davis told us everything—I've been worried all afternoon—"

"Mom, stop—I'm okay!" Christie said, wrenching her face out of her mom's shoulder just to talk. "Seriously, look at me! I'm all right."

Mercifully, Mrs. Cunningham did so, letting go of her daughter and looking her up and down. "You need to wear your glasses, hon—at least for your right eye. You have no peripherals otherwise."

Christie's gaze dropped. "People will point and stare if I wear them with just one lens in."

"We'll get them fixed soon, sweetheart—don't worry," she said in a softer tone. Then she turned her attention to Zech. "And who's this?"

"Oh!" Christie said, jumping at the opportunity. "Mom, this is Zechariah Forshaw—the one who defended me from Trace."

"Oh!" Mrs. Cunningham's eyebrows shot up. Then she blinked like she was fighting back tears. "Thank you, Zechariah," she said. "You have no idea how much this means to us. Why don't you come in and have a glass of cider? Christie's grandma has some brownies in the oven, too, if you'd like."

Zech's mouth watered. "Thank you, Mrs. Cunningham.

I'd *love* to stop in—I really would. But my mom will be home any minute, so I should probably be going."

Mrs. Cunningham smiled. "Of course. I'll put something together for you to take home with you."

Zech smiled nervously. "Okay—thank you!"

Mrs. Cunningham nodded, then led the way down a short hall, through an eating area, and into a living room with a plush green leather love seat and a black leather recliner right next to it. "Have a seat, Zech, and I'll send you on your way," Mrs. Cunningham said, gesturing at the recliner.

Zech nodded and obliged, while Christie perched herself on the small couch, her legs folded under her crisscross-applesauce. Gratitude and warmth overflowed in him as he took in the kindness and compassion. Then, his stomach flipped as he asked, "Hey, Christie? Would you still be up for a study session sometime?"

Christie's eyes lit up. "Yes! I mean, I'll check with my parents, but I'd be happy to study with you!"

Zech had to temper his smile, but fireworks were going off in his head. "Great! Keep me posted," he managed.

"Absolutely." They shook on it, both trying to mask their excitement.

CHAPTER 10

THE SCROLL UNSEALED

"So you're telling me," Caleb said, eyeing the gray-bearded elder seated before him, "that there's a prophecy in these Holy Scrolls about *me?*"

The old man smiled, eyes twinkling. "You—or someone just *like* you, my son."

Caleb frowned dubiously. "You really think I could fulfill any of these prophecies, sir—with all due respect?"

Elder Michael's face sobered. "Tell me, Caleb—do you believe, with all your heart, in the words which Sister Charis sang about the Anointed Lord upon your meeting?"

Caleb hesitated. "I do and I don't. One of your fellow monks explained it well enough, and I *think* I believe it—but there's still so much I don't understand!"

To his surprise, Elder Michael's smile returned. "That will come in due time, my son. A humble heart matters more to our Lord than what men call wisdom. Trust in Him and His finished work, and all shall be well with your spirit. You can trust our Lord's faithfulness—proven in every word our scribes have carefully copied and preserved."

Caleb drew a breath. "Yes, I think I believe. But what's all this got to do with *me,* sir?"

"Ah! At the beginning of the kingdom, the seer Esmeralda prophesied: 'An heir shall come to restore the kingdom, bearing the Stone that was lost, at a time when the realm is bereaved and under great duress, besieged, dogged by foes as sheep among wolves. Most did not understand this saying, but as Ilamar grew and prospered, those who studied the Scrolls viewed it as a provision should the worst come to pass. After all, how could Ilamar fall with the Lord's blessing upon it? Yet in the year you were born, the queen's heir was lost—and the Stone with him. Then many began to see how the prophecy might unfold, and their hopes rose that its fulfillment was near. But as time wore on, such hopes waned. And *you,* my son Caleb, bear the very name the queen gave her heir—though you look it not."

"And how do you know it's me, sir?"

Elder Michael fixed him with a firm gaze. "The Stone."

Caleb's eyes widened. "The Stone I found? *That's* what Sister Charis meant in her vision?"

"Yes! It is both the heirloom and heir-illuminator of Ilamar. Only the true heir can hold it aglow without being burned, and if any try to seize it wrongfully, it would burn like a coal till he drops it. Thus only the heir may return it to the palace and assume the throne."

Caleb was flabbergasted. Could any of this really be true of *him*? Finally, he managed, "What must I do *now,* Elder?"

"The only thing *to* be done, my son—you must go to Castle Ilamar and present yourself to Their Majesties."

Caleb's stomach lurched. "Me? Go to the castle? But I can't go alone!"

"Nay, my liege. You shall not be alone. Sister Charis, myself, and one of our knights will accompany you—and guide you in the Way of our Master, as all Ilamari ought to be."

"But sir, what if they don't believe me?"

"Trust in God, my dear prince, and He will make straight your paths."

* * *

"Well, class, here are your homework packets from Monday," Mrs. Davis said. "Kalina, would you pass these out, please?"

"What'd you get?" Zech asked Eddie.

"C," Eddie muttered, stifling a yawn. "You?"

Zech braced for the worst—but saw far fewer red marks than expected. The corrections felt almost . . . gentle. At the bottom, Mrs. Davis had written something he never thought he'd see:

85/100 (B)
Well done!

His jaw dropped. Since sophomore year, he couldn't remember anything higher than a C—outside of lifting.

"Hey! You awake?"

"Good." Zech shrugged.

Eddie squinted. "Really, bro? What'd you get?"

Zech gulped. "Eighty-five."

"What?!" Eddie nearly leapt from his chair. "No way—that's cap! Gimme that!"

"Hey!"

Too late. Eddie snatched the packet, stared, then smirked. In a mocking falsetto, he repeated, "'Well done!' Well, look at you, teacher's pet!"

"That's not fair!" Zech hissed. "It's no big deal, and it's none of your business what Mrs. Davis thinks of my work."

"*Work!* Bro, you *barely* scrape by with a C. Then suddenly you're too good for me, you throw yourself in front of *Trace Seamore,* and now you're kissing up to the *teacher?* Nah, man—some'm' up with you, an' I don't like it!"

"Well, sorry you don't like it, then! And I'm sorry I pushed you away earlier—I was in a bad spot. But I'm not acting better than you—because I'm really*not!* I just wanna do the right thing."

"Well, whoop-dee-doo, Mr. Goody Two-Shoes—"

A sharp kick hit their chairs. "Shush!" Christie hissed. "Mrs. Davis is talking!"

"Mrs. Davis is talking!" Eddie jeered.

"Shut *up,* Eddie!" Zech spat. "You're being stupid, and you know it!"

"Oh yeah? Whatcha gonna do, big shot?"

"Is everything okay back there?" Mrs. Davis' voice cut through.

They froze, and Zech and Eddie glared daggers at

each other. Then Zech dropped his gaze. "Sorry, Mrs. Davis. Everything's fine."

"Teacher's pet," Eddie muttered.

Zech ignored him.

* * *

"All right! Get to it, gents!"

Coach Brent Limbaugh watched his class prep for leg day, always on the alert for slackers. Standards mattered—if they couldn't adhere to them, then you better believe he would let them know.

"Hey, Coach?"

Brent pivoted. There stood Zechariah Forshaw, nervous but steady. "Something to say, Forshaw?"

"Yes." The boy's voice wavered, but held. "I'm sorry about before. What I said was stupid, and what I was doing was worse. I understand now—homework first, and do our best with everything. I hope you can forgive me."

Brent blinked. This was almost too perfect! "You mean that, Forshaw?"

"Absolutely, sir," Zech said, his voice firmer and more resolute than Brent remembered.

Brent studied him. Something about the boy had changed, *that* was for sure. "Got that in writing, Forshaw?" he asked, raising an eyebrow.

Zech startled, then smiled nervously. "I wondered if you'd say that." He pulled a small envelope from his pocket.

Brent tore it open. The note said much the same as his

apology. Then warm pride welled in him. *Looks like he's finally got it through his thick skull.*

"Tell ya what, kid," Brent said, pocketing the note. "By the time you change, class will be over. But I expect to see you with the rest of those yahoos on Monday. Got it?"

Zech smiled. "Yes, sir!"

"Good! You're free to go. And Forshaw?"

"Yes, sir?"

"I'm proud of you, son."

* * *

Bethany Sinclair rifled through her school mailbox, as she did each week. Usually, it was just junk or paperwork, but occasionally she received letters from alumni. Today, she found a single envelope, with a slender object inside. Curious, she carried it to her car, opened it, and read:

Dear Ms. Sinclair,

Hi. It's Zechariah Forshaw. I was in your class last year. I don't know if you remember, but I stole this red Sharpie from you. I always saw you marking so many of my answers wrong. But I've had a radical life change after finding the Messiah, and now I'm giving it back. I'm sorry, and I hope you can forgive me. Have a great weekend.

From,
Zech

Bethany stared in bewilderment at the letter and the

marker. Yes, she *had* missed it once, but eventually she'd forgotten about it. But now, with this apology, she felt truly touched. Zech came flooding back to mind—rough edges and all. She resolved to write him back, praying she'd find a way to deliver it. Then she put her car in drive and headed home.

CHAPTER 11

THE SUNDAY STUDY SESSION

"So will you be lifting again tomorrow?" Christie asked, leaning across the small table Mike Stroud had lent them.

"I think so," Zech said.

"Good for you! Looks like things are starting to turn around."

Zech frowned. "Sorry about Eddie. I should've apologized to him sooner—I don't know where that came from."

"He'll come around," Christie said. "How long have you known each other?"

Zech shrugged. "Six, seven years. Not long after my dad left."

"Oh." Her beautiful face fell. "I'm sorry—I didn't mean to—"

"No, no! You're good!" An awkward silence settled over them, and Zech felt awful for causing it. "So," he said, nodding at the homework packets between them, "where should we start?"

Christie's gaze snapped back to the present. "Right. What do you need the most help with?"

"Math, but I hate it!" Zech smirked.

Christie laughed, and his heart lurched at the sound. "All the more reason to get crackin'! Which math?"

"Algebra 2."

"Okay. That's not terrible!"

"It's the hardest math *I've* ever done."

"Not as hard as calculus, trust me!"

"You take *calculus?*"

"Uh-huh."

Zech whistled. "You're gonna need a different study partner for *that!*"

She laughed again, her cheek dimpling as her smile reached her eyes. "Let's get started, funny boy!"

Blushing, Zech grabbed a folder to hide his face. "Right."

Christie moved to his side, and they began. As they worked, Zech noticed she would either hold the papers close or squint at them. He didn't recall her doing that before.

"Hey, Christie?" he asked about twenty minutes in.

"Hmm?" She turned to him.

"You're squinting a lot. Glasses giving you trouble? Or do I just have terrible handwriting?" he added with a smirk.

Christie's face went pale, sending a chill through him. Then she forced a smile. "I'll be fine once I get my glasses replaced."

Uneasy, Zech nodded, and they returned to work.

Two half-hour sessions later—with a break in between—Zech's brain felt like mush, but he felt a bit more confident. "Thanks a bunch, Christie! I don't know if I'll *remember* it all, but I think I get *some* of it now."

"Happy to help. And hey, something's better than nothing, right?"

"I hope so—or I'm a dead man come Thursday!" he said with a grin.

"You'll do just fine. Just study your notes, pray, and do your best."

"I'll try," he said, still queasy at the thought of the exam. Guess that's all anyone's ever expected of me, huh?"

"I'm sure you will. I believe in you. I'll be praying."

"Thank you," Zech managed, his voice catching. Standing up, he led the way downstairs, where Mike waited with Christie's mother.

"Well, hello there!" Mike greeted with a jovial smile. "Was your studying productive?"

"Yes, sir!" Zech said just as Christie chimed in, "Yes, thank you!" They glanced at each other in surprise.

"Excellent! What did you work on?"

"Math," they said together, and glanced at each other again.

"Very good. I don't fully understand the math you kids are learning these days—but math itself is always worth learning."

Zech shrugged. "Not sure when *I'll* ever use Algebra 2, but I'll apply myself."

"You never know," Mike said, winking.

"I guess," Zech said, then turned to Christie's mother. "Thanks for letting us work here, Mrs. Cunningham."

"Anytime, Zech," she said with a smile. "Christie loves

study sessions. I'm glad she has a partner who's as interested in school as she is."

Zech blushed at the word *partner*. "It's my pleasure," he managed, pretending to scrutinize the books on the shelf beside him.

"Mine too!" Christie said, her voice brightened by her smile. "See you tomorrow!"

"See ya tomorrow!" Zech said, catching her eye as she and her mom left. "Bye, Christie! Bye, Mrs. Cunningham! Thanks for everything!"

"You're welcome!" Christie called back as the door clicked shut, the bell tingling overhead.

"Something up, Zech?"

"What?" He whirled around to find Mike watching him.

"You were staring out the door like a lost puppy!"

Zech's face burned. "I'm fine, Mr. Stroud, really."

Mike studied him a moment, then said, "All right. If you say so. Well, see you tomorrow!"

"Yup!"

Mortified, Zech slipped outside—only to spot Corban's faded cherry-red Toyota idling at the curb. His brother honked twice and waved. Zech returned the wave and climbed into the back seat. "Hey!"

"Hey, little bro!" Corban said cheerfully as they pulled away. Catching Zech's expression in the mirror, he explained, "*Imma* asked me to pick you up."

Oh! So, Mom's still at the hospital?"

"Yeah, she said some last-minute stuff came up and couldn't make it back till late."

"Gotcha." Zech glanced at the passenger seat. "Where's Olivia?"

"Homework. She wanted to make a dent in chemistry. But we've got plans tonight, so it's not *all* bad."

"Cool." Zech felt awkwardness rising within him like a thick ooze. "Hey, Corban?"

"Yeah?"

"Can I ask you something—personal?"

"Sure! What's up?"

Zech hesitated, then blurted, "How did you know Olivia was the one?"

Corban was quiet for a long moment. "I guess what worked for me may not be the same for everyone. But I liked her the moment I saw her—she was pretty, smart, funny. As I got to know her, I really fell in love. Over time I began to see a future with her. We went to church and synagogue together, met each other's families, studied, prayed, fought, forgave—and I realized there was no one else I'd rather spend my life with."

"So what did you do to make it happen?"

"I didn't," Corban said matter-of-factly, giving Zech a reproachful look. "I prayed, sought God's will, and made sure we were equally yoked—both believers with the same values. The rest was up to God."

Zech turned away sheepishly. "It's just—" He cut himself off.

"Go on," Corban urged.

"Nah, it's okay—never mind."

"No, it's not—or you wouldn't have asked. Come on. Tell me. I promise I won't tell *Imma*."

"So," with a sigh, Zech explained, "there's this girl at school I really like, but we only started talking a week or two ago, and I don't know what to do."

Corban thought a moment. "Is she a believer?"

"Yes!" Zech said quickly. "And so am I now—"

Corban nearly swerved into the oncoming lane. "Dude! Why didn't you say that *first*? That's amazing! Hallelujah!"

Zech blushed, but smiled. "Sorry. Guess I didn't think to tell you. But yeah, I believe in Jesus now."

"Praise God! That's awesome! And great that she's a believer too; that's a *huge* green flag."

"I know, but—"

"It's complicated."

"Something like that."

"Well, let's start with the positives: What do you like about her?"

"She's pretty, smart, funny, and gets good grades. She's also dedicated, hardworking, and willing to help. We just spent an hour in Imagine Nation doing math homework together."

"Great!"

"But . . ."

"But?"

"She's got bad eyesight, and I don't know how to handle it—especially since I've got a crush on her."

Corban nodded. "Is it degenerative, or has she always had bad eyesight?"

"I don't know. She never specified, but today I saw her squinting even with her glasses, so something is definitely up."

"Well, would it be your business to know that?"

"I guess not. But I'm worried about *her*. Besides"—he smirked—"how can she help me with homework if I can't understand it and she can't read *it?*"

Corban laughed. "Touché. But don't let that stop you. Bad eyesight doesn't change who she is."

Zech frowned. "It's not *that* so much as the fact that she won't talk about it when it seems important. Mr. Stroud told me she'd tell me in her own time. Even today, when I asked, she just blamed her glasses—but I know she used to read the board from farther away."

Corban thought, then nodded. "Sorry, little bro, but I think Mr. Stroud's got a point. The best thing you can do is wait until she's ready—and *pray for her*. The one exception would be if it's obvious something's wrong and she brushes it off. Then ask gently, as a friend."

Zech's gut twisted. "As a friend?"

"Yes. If this is meant to blossom, nourish your friendship with her first. Learn who she is as a person—her quirks, her hopes, her fears. And pray, pray, pray. If God intends it, He'll make it happen. But if you try to force it, it won't go the way you hope."

Zech let Corban's words sink in. Finally, he said, "I don't like it. But I understand."

"Take it slow, bro, and pray about it. If it's meant to be, it will be." Then he laughed nervously.

"You good, bro?" Zech asked.

"Yeah," Corban said, his expression shifting to nervous excitement. "It's funny, though. I was planning on proposing to Olivia tonight."

"Whoa! Congrats!"

"Thanks. It's just that talking to you reminded me why I love her—and why this is so nerve-racking and beautiful." He smiled warmly. "Thanks, little bro. I needed that."

"No prob. Thanks yourself, big bro."

"Anytime. And don't tell *Imma*—you know the drill] about Olivia, okay? We'll tell her when we're ready."

"Gotcha. Think she'll say yes?"

"I think so. I *hope* so. Pray for me, Zech."

"I will. And you, too, Corban."

"I will. We *both* will—if that's okay."

"Yeah. Yeah, that'd be great."

* * *

"So, how did it go?" Christie's mom asked as they pulled out of the lot.

"Good!" Christie said. "We got through a lot, and I think he understands it better now."

"Good," her mom said, staring straight ahead.

"Mom? Is something wrong?"

Her mom cocked an eyebrow. "Sorry, honey. I was just thinking. This was Zechariah Forshaw, right?" Christie nodded. "Wasn't he one of the boys you used to say were obnoxious in class?"

"Well, yeah, but he's changed a *lot!*"

"I just wondered if he'd be a difficult study partner."

"No, I get it," Christie said with a nod. "Honestly, I wasn't sure what to expect either. But he really *has* changed! Two weeks ago, he wanted nothing to do with me—he initially balked at my offer of help, and I only did it because it was the right thing to do. But later he admitted that he did need help and apologized—and you know he saved me from Trace Seamore."

Her mother's gaze softened. "That really *was* a great thing he did." After a pause, she asked, "What do you think of him?"

Christie blinked. "What do you mean?"

"As a person. What do you make of him?"

Christie thought for a moment. "Well, like I said, he's changed. I used to see him as just a swaggering jock who didn't care about school. But now . . . I think there's potential. He's opened himself to come to Christ, and he wants to learn. He's still coming out of his shell, but from what I've seen, he's brave, intelligent, curious—and doesn't suffer fools."

"What do you mean by that?"

"Well, he and Eddie—the other boy I've told you about—used to tease me all the time about being a teacher's pet. But last Friday, he stood up for me *against* Eddie, which surprised me. And"—she almost giggled—"he's funnier than I thought—in a dry, self-deprecating way. He joked that I'd need a different study partner for calc, and it made me laugh." She met her mom's eyes. "I know it's early, but I think I could consider him a friend."

"Hmm." Her mother looked pensive again.

"What?" Christie asked, her gut twisting. "What do *you* think of him?"

"I haven't known him long enough. I'm glad *you* like him. I'd just like to get to know him better myself."

Christie relaxed. "That makes sense. Could we invite him to church sometime?"

"Doesn't he go somewhere?"

"Yeah, the Davises' house for synagogue."

"Synagogue?"

"Yeah."

"I thought you said he found Christ."

"Oh, he has!"

"Oh!" Her mother looked genuinely surprised. "I guess there's no harm in inviting him for a Sunday. And if Miss Ema's okay with it, you could go to her place sometime too."

"I'm good with either," Christie said with relief. "Can we still do study sessions at Imagine Nation?"

"Of course. Oh, and honey? I've set up an appointment for new glasses tomorrow at 3:15. Wait for me in the lobby after school."

Christie's heart leapt. "Really? Thank you, Mom!"

"No problem. And just so you know, the offer still stands if you want to—"

"That's okay, Mom."

"Are you sure? Mr. Stroud could help find someone who—"

"I'm fine, Mom, but thanks."

Her mother looked surprised, then nodded. "Okay, hon. I just thought I'd offer."

CHAPTER 12

LIGHT AND SHADOW

Things began to look up for Zech as October wore on. He rejoined lifting and continued saving his wages from Imagine Nation. The Tuesday after their first study session, he was glad to see Christie sporting a brand-new pair of glasses, with a more durable frame and thicker lenses.

"As if she didn't look like a big enough nerd already," Eddie scoffed.

"I think they're great," Zech said, ignoring him. "Hope they work for you."

And for a little while, they seemed to. The study sessions continued, Zech's grades climbed, and he even began receiving accolades from his teachers. To his relief, he managed a ninety on the math quiz—a grade that he hadn't seen since middle school. (Lifting was a pass/fail.)

But as the weeks passed, Zech began to worry. Christie started glancing at her notes more often, squinting at the board, and frowning in concentration. Mrs. Davis must have noticed, too, because around Columbus Day she reshuffled the seating, moving Zech to the second row and Christie to the front. Christie looked embarrassed, but she adjusted quickly and was soon thriving.

But to his horror, the old signs returned. Christie stared harder and harder at the board, wiped her lenses frequently, and gradually stopped taking notes. Zech offered to let her borrow his notes, and she accepted, but even so—she participated less and less, her answers clipped and hesitant. A shadow seemed to settle over her—one Zech felt powerless to banish. Church and synagogue gave her a temporary glow, but in class, the darkness returned.

By Halloween Thursday, the whole school was decked out—with fake cobwebs, skeletons, and pumpkins everywhere. Motion-activated decorations shrieked and cackled as people walked by. Zech found them more corny than scary—though the candy in every classroom was a plus.

English class, however, felt routine—until Zech noticed Christie staring blankly at the board, her pen poised but unmoving. Halfway through, she took off her glasses, polished them, and put them back on. She glanced at the board, then at her empty paper, then back at the board. Then, to his shock, she stood, turned, and headed for the door, bumping into desks and legs along the way and earning irritated looks from classmates. At last, she burst through the door and fled into the hallway.

For a moment, there was silence, and Zech began to wonder whether he should go check on her. Then, from the hallway, came a bloodcurdling scream. Zech shot to his feet, with Mrs. Davis hot on his heels as he charged from the room.

In the hallway, they found Christie crumpled on the floor, sobbing. A motion-activated skeleton leered over her, its eyes glowing as it thundered, shrieked, and cackled—finishing with a sinister, "Happy Halloween!" Zech's fists clenched; he felt a powerful urge to smash the stupid decoration in its bony, plastic face. But he wrangled his emotions, forcing his attention back to Christie.

"Are you all right?" Mrs. Davis asked, kneeling and stroking her goddaughter's hair. "Are you hurt?"

Christie shook her head, but couldn't speak yet.

"It's all right, sweetheart," Mrs. Davis said gently. "I can go get the nurse if you want."

Christie sniffed so sharply that it sounded more like a choke. "No, Miss Ema, I'm f-fine. Y-you should get back to class. I—I just need a minute."

Her godmother hesitated.

"It's all right, Mrs. Davis," Zech said. "I'll stay with her—make sure she's okay."

Mrs. Davis blinked, then nodded, patted Christie's back, and returned to class.

Left alone, Zech fidgeted. *What was he supposed to do?* He couldn't comfort Christie the way her godmother had—but he had to do *something.* Finally, he asked, "Hey, you okay? What happened?"

Christie buried her face in her hands and sobbed harder.

"What's wrong?" he tried again, instantly regretting it as she dissolved further. At that, he decided silence was safer. "Come on," he said at last, helping her to her feet.

"Thanks," she choked out.

They walked to the commons, where Zech chose a corner away from the hallways. He sat her down, waiting awkwardly as she wept. To his surprise, the walk had steadied her, and she soon settled, staring at the table.

At length, he asked again, "Christie, what's wrong?"

She turned halfheartedly and said, "I can't see."

Immediately, Zech's stomach dropped. He'd feared it was her eyes—but nothing quite *this* bad. "What do you mean?"

She drew a long breath. "I have a degenerative eye condition—congenital retinal dystrophy. Basically, I was born with retinas that were doomed to deteriorate and fail. My right eye's been going for a while, but my left compensated. That's why I could read with one broken lens. But now . . ." Her voice faltered. "I've lost *all* vision in my right eye, and my left is failing fast. All I see is fog—thick, gray fog. Nothing else!" Her face twisted in anguish. "I knew this would happen eventually, but I always thought I'd have more time. Why does this have to happen now? Why—when I should be moving forward—does everything stop? I'll never see my family, my friends, the birds in the apple tree, the blossoms, the books. I'll never read or write again! And if I can't do *that*, what's the point of anything?" At that, she dissolved into tears again.

Zech's mind spun. Nothing he could say felt right. *I'm sorry. Can I pray for you? How can I help?* Each sounded inadequate. So he sat quietly, praying silently.

Lord God, I'm really gonna need Your help with this one!

* * *

Zech let out a weary, relieved sigh as Mike Stroud ushered the last costumed child out of the store. The clock read 11:03 p.m. Outside, the shrieks of trick-or-treaters, the cold draft each time the door opened, the bell's constant ring, the late hour, and the gnawing question of how to help Christie all pressed on him. Yet, with Mike tasking him with stocking books, Zech thanked God he had memorized the system well enough to work almost on autopilot.

"There," Mike said, satisfied. Just one or two more things, and we'll close for the night."

Zech yawned as Mike settled behind the desk and began typing. Suddenly, a terrible clattering rattled the room, making Zech jump.

"Oh—sorry, Zech," Mike said. "I forgot to tell you about the embosser."

"The *what?*"

"The embosser. It makes Braille. I'm starting a Braille production line to make my books available to more people."

Zech froze. "Oh. Wait, Braille? As in the dots on bathroom signs? Blind people can read that?"

Mike smiled. "Yes. It's actually required by law for many places to have Braille signage. That's how people with little to no vision can read what sighted people see instantly."

"And you say it works for books too?"

"Of course! I'll probably add shelves downstairs just for Braille." He eyed Zech curiously. "Why do you ask, son?"

"Oh, just curious," Zech said.

Mike narrowed his eyes.

Zech sighed. No use hiding it. "Christie told me about her vision."

Mike's brows rose. "Oh?" he asked, coming out from behind the desk and facing him. "She hasn't mentioned it to me in some time."

"It's bad," Zech said solemnly. "I won't get into details that aren't mine to share, but she can't read either my notes or the board anymore. But this Braille—this might be the answer I've been praying for!"

Mike's expression darkened. "Christie may not be very open to learning Braille."

"What? Why not?"

"Well, many see it as strange or niche—'that thing that blind people read.' And it takes time to learn—time she might fear will cost her grades."

Zech sagged. How could he ask her to learn something she already resented? Then a wild idea struck him—bold and clear. "Then I'll learn it with her."

Mike's eyes widened. "You would?"

"Sure. If I learn, she won't feel so alone. Besides, how can I help *her* learn it if *I* don't know it myself?"

Mike studied him for a long moment, then smiled, clapping his shoulder. "That might just work. I'll be praying for you both."

"Thank you, sir," Zech said quietly. *I'll need it.*

"And Zech?"

"Yes, sir?"

"I'm proud of the young man you're becoming, son."

Zech smiled sheepishly. "Guess I've got good role models lately."

"Oh? And whom might those be?"

"Well, Caleb and Elder Michael from your book—so basically you—my brother, Corban, and Jesus Messiah Himself."

Mike chuckled. "Well, I'm humbled that you see fit to include me on that list—if indirectly. But tell me: what do all those people represent to you?"

Zech thought for a moment, then said, "Humility, wisdom, and chivalry. Gentle with friends, restrained when provoked, but dangerous to those who threaten their loved ones. Even willing to lay down their lives for them—Messiah most of all."

Mike nodded, eyes warm. "You've grown, Zech. I pray that you become that sort of man—and more!"

CHAPTER 13

LEARNING BY FEEL

Christie hated being led around. Ever since she had come home and confessed the horror to her parents, they'd made her hold on to their arms whenever they went anywhere together. She'd grudgingly allowed Zech to help her—at least to the classes they shared—but the humiliation still gnawed at her. All day long, her parents' words rang through her head: "If you want to continue doing well in school, you've got to advocate for yourself in the classroom, and you've got to learn to read Braille. We're willing to help get everything set up for you, but you have to want it for yourself." Those words galled her.

By now, her Sunday study sessions with Zech had become routine, but she was so down in the dumps that she nearly skipped after church. The preacher had preached from 2 Corinthians 5, and Christie had bristled at the imagery. *But what's the point of living in a tent if you can't see out the windows?* Yet his explanation of verse 7—"For we walk by faith and not by sight,"—had taken the initial sting out of it. Instead of shame, she felt a strange sense of encouragement. Zech had promised on Friday that he was committed to helping her in any way he could. If nothing else, she figured she'd go for the company—even if she couldn't read his or anyone else's handwriting anymore.

And so it was that she found herself in the lobby of Imagine Nation as her mother kissed her cheek and left. Christie stood, confused and apprehensive, wondering where everyone was and what was coming next. But she wasn't left standing alone for long.

"Christie!" Mike said jovially. He shook her hand, then offered his arm. "I'm glad you could come."

"Hey, Christie!" Zech called from somewhere nearby—Christie wished she could see exactly where.

"Hi," she said uncertainly. "What's up?"

Zech hesitated, tension thick in the air. Finally, he said, "You remember how I told you I'm committed to helping you no matter what?"

"Yes," she said with a nod.

"Well, Mr. Mike and I think we have an idea. I—we, I mean—know how much reading means to you. Mr. Mike wanted to branch out in the formats of books he sells, so we thought we'd try killing two birds with one stone."

Christie cocked an eyebrow. "What do you mean?"

"Come here," Mike said, guiding her over to the checkout desk. He placed her hand on something hard, flat, and plastic. Feeling along its edges, she discovered that it was about eight and a half by eleven inches square, with a solid plastic binder secured by about twenty-five plastic rings looped through the spine.

Her eyes went wide. "Is this a book?" she asked, feeling the thickness and hefting it in her hands. "It's huge!"

"Yep!" Mike said. "The prototype Braille edition of *The Stone of Ilamar.*"

"Oh." Christie's heart sank.

"Mike was thinking about adding a Braille section to the store," Zech explained. "And after the other day, I thought—"

"That I should learn Braille?" Christie asked dryly, her heart slipping beneath the carpet. "Yeah, I know. My mom's been after me to start—"

"Christie," Mike said, a gentle edge in his voice, "let him finish."

Her cheeks burned. "Sorry, Zech."

"It's all right," Zech said, still nervous. "Well, I was thinking—given your . . . condition—maybe we could learn it. Together."

Her breath caught. *"We?* But why?"

"That way you won't be struggling alone."

Christie frowned. "But you can see the letters."

"Not if I close my eyes."

Despite herself, Christie snorted. "You don't have to do that!"

"No, but I *can*—just to even the playing field."

"You'll look like a fool!"

"Maybe. But if it helps you, so be it."

Christie was floored. Had Zech read her mind? Or had Mr. Stroud coached him? Either way, the plan seemed to mollify nearly all her insecurities—with a few notable exceptions.

"But what about schoolwork?" she asked. "I can't help you anymore, and I won't be able to do mine until I learn this."

"Ema told me there are ways to get help—teacher aides, note-takers, and the like," Mike said. "All you have to do is ask."

Christie sighed, both reluctant and relieved. Her parents were right. She hated admitting it—but oh, the weight that lifted! "All right," she said. "How do we start?"

"Come with me," Mike said. "Since you're both going in blind—literally—we'll start in the Dark Room. An old friend left me his Braille learning tools."

Curious, Christie took Zech's elbow and followed Mike upstairs. Zech guided her into a chair, then sat beside her. She squinted at the gray column of smoke—that was all she could see of the candle—as Mike rummaged for something.

"Ah, here it is!" he said, shaking what sounded like game pieces. "Feel on the table, just in front of you."

Christie's fingers touched a small rectangular piece of wood with six raised pegs—three rows of two.

"What's this?" Zech asked.

"This is a representation of one Braille cell," Mike explained. "Each cell can stand for one or more characters, depending on the dot combinations."

He explained the numbering, then started walking them through the alphabet. Christie couldn't quite detect a pattern yet, but drilling herself on the pegs made the letters easier than expected. Zech looked eager but puzzled, clearly trying to find a system—until he realized he was better off simply listening.

"Trust me, Zech," Mike said. "You'll notice patterns soon enough. But we'll keep it simple today. I don't want to overwhelm you by throwing too much at you."

And so he did—until their brains felt spent. "We should do this again sometime," Zech said.

"I agree!" Christie said, surprising herself. "Maybe I'll actually be able to read your book soon!"

Mike chuckled. "How do Sundays and Wednesdays sound?"

"Perfect!" they chorused.

"Excellent!" Mike said jovially. "I'll check with your parents, but I'm sure it'll be fine."

With that, Zech helped her back down to the lobby, where her mother was waiting for her. Upon her departure, Christie mulled it over. Zech's devotion touched her. Learning Braille hadn't been nearly as humiliating as she'd feared. She even looked forward to their next lesson—to seeing him again. But one thing remained.

"Hey, Mom?" she asked.

"Yes, dear?"

"Would you please ask the school for someone to help me with my work? I don't know how it'd work, since I can't read anymore—but could you at least ask?"

"Of course, sweetheart," her mother said, a smile in her voice.

CHAPTER 14

UNDER FIRE

"All right, class," Mrs. Davis said. "We've finished *Fahrenheit 451!*" A few people clapped—Christie among them. "Now it's time for your midterm group projects. I want you to put yourself in Montag's shoes at the end of the book. Was everything you've done worth it? Why or why not? And what do you plan to do from here? You may present your work in either written or recorded form. Papers must be at least three pages; videos or recordings, at least three minutes. You may upload to social media if everyone consents and the content is appropriate. I've assigned your groups, so I'll pass the lists around with the rubric. Projects are due the day before Thanksgiving break. Use the rest of class to plan. Good luck!"

Zech groaned inwardly. He trusted himself to work hard, but his old notes weren't reliable. If he paired with Christie, maybe they could manage—but her notes were now useless to her.

When Mrs. Davis came to Christie, she leaned in and whispered something. Immediately, Christie's face blanched, and Zech's stomach dropped.

"What is it?" he whispered.

"You'll see," Christie whispered back.

His heart raced as he scanned his packet: *Christie Cunningham, Zechariah Forshaw, and Edward Longshore.*

"What?!" he whisper-yelled.

"Shhh!" Christie hissed.

Warily, Zech obliged, though he watched Eddie's eyes go wide—then narrow in disgust—as he read his own packet. He shot Zech a look that screamed, *You gotta be kidding me!*

"Well, ain't this just my lucky day!" Eddie sneered, plopping down beside them.

"Look, Eddie, I'm not exactly over the moon about this either," Zech said, "but let's just try to make the best of it."

"The best of what?" Eddie retorted. "One of us can't even read or write at the moment. Feels like Mrs. Davis set us up to fail."

"She wouldn't," Christie said firmly.

"Oh yeah? Then why put us together, *professor?*" Eddie asked.

"Well," Christie said carefully, "maybe we should start with our strengths. I used to take detailed notes—we can use those."

"If anyone can *read* them," Eddie muttered.

"Are you volunteering?" Zech shot back.

Eddie shrugged. "If I gave a hairy rat's behind about all this, maybe I would."

Zech glared. "What is your problem?"

"You know what," Eddie growled.

"Guys, stop, please!" Christie pleaded. "What happened to teamwork?"

"We had teamwork?" Zech asked sarcastically.

"We'll need it if we want above a B-plus," she said.

Eddie snorted. "That'd be a miracle."

"Why?" Zech snapped. "Because of us, or because of you?"

The words hung in the air. Eddie's chair crashed and clattered backward as he lunged at Zech, fist raised. Zech ducked, bracing to strike—

"Boys!" Mrs. Davis barked. "Sit down," she said sternly. They did.

"Now, I don't care who started it. You're both better than that. Take a breath and start over, or *you two* are going to the office. Understand?"

They nodded. Zech's cheeks burned.

"Good." Mrs. Davis walked back to her desk.

"Sorry," Zech said to Christie. "She's right."

Christie shrugged. "Don't apologize to *me*. I'm fine!"

"Right." Zech turned to Eddie. "Sorry. That was out of line."

"Sure. Whatever." Eddie mumbled something that sounded a lot like "*sellout.*"

Frustrated, Zech huffed. "So what do we do?"

Christie thought for a moment, then perked up and turned to Eddie. "You like making music videos, right?"

Eddie blinked. "How'd *you* know that?" he asked, astonished.

"I used to overhear you and Zech talking about them way back when. What if we did something like that?"

Eddie frowned. "What, a *Fahrenheit 451* rap?" he asked dubiously.

"Sounds pretty fire to *me,*" Zech said dryly.

Both Christie and Eddie tried to hold back a laugh. Finally, Eddie cracked a smile. "Right on!"

Christie giggled. "Sorry. That caught me off guard. But yes—let's do a rap video. What *would* we do in Montag's situation?"

* * *

By the end of class, they had a plan. Zech would compile his and Christie's notes into a Google Doc, and Eddie would draw lyrics from it. From there, his creative gears would start turning, shaping slam poetry that would torch Montag's enemies—within PG limits, of course.

Later, on the bus, Eddie overheard Christie laughing again—only the second time he'd ever heard it.

Is he rizzin' her up? Eddie wondered. But then he saw Zech relaxed in a way he hadn't seen since they were younger. He'd been bitter as Zech had shunted him aside in favor of Christie, and Eddie could hardly see how those two would ever mesh. But hearing them now, he realized how different the two seemed. Maybe Christie really did bring out the best in him—just as Eddie had brought out the worst in him after Mr. Forshaw left.

"So, how's work?" Christie asked.

"Oh, same as always." Zech shrugged. "Mike bumped my rate to thirty!" He smirked. "Think he's tryin' to get rid of me faster?"

"No!" Christie laughed, elbowing him in the ribs. "He likes you. Will you be off for Veterans Day?"

"Yeah. He and his family are doing the parade. And I'm off Thanksgiving too. He'll open for Black Friday sales, but he's not expecting much. He *does* hope to have some Braille books ready by then—though he needs more staff to proofread. Actually"—he smirked again—"kinda made me think of you."

Christie laughed louder. "Yeah, right. The kid who can only read from *A to J* in Braille proofreading entire books."

"No, I'm serious! Reading and correcting typos in books all day? That sounds like Heaven for you!"

She elbowed him a little harder. "You're making fun of me! Quit it!"

Zech laughed. "Am I wrong, though?"

Christie shrugged, pretending to pout, though Eddie thought he saw a dimple in her cheek.

Eddie shook his head, surprised at his own thoughts. *Let 'em have their fun. They look happy.*

Eddie's stop came after Zech's and Christie's, and he was always the only one to get off there. Just as he turned toward his house, someone stepped in his way. Startled, Eddie looked up to find Trace Seamore glaring at him.

"Wait till the bus leaves," Trace said, voice low and cold.

Eddie complied, then squared up—chest out, shoulders back. "Whadda you want, Trace?"

"Just a friendly chat," Trace said with a sharkish smile. He looked different since his suspension—buzzed hair, sharper muscles; older, meaner, and more intense.

"What about?" Eddie asked, forcing a mask of indifference.

"You an' Forshaw were close, right?"

Eddie's stomach sank. "We *used* to be," he said stiffly. "What's up with you anyway? You goin' to the Army recruiter or some'm?"

Trace laughed cruelly. "Me? Go to *those* chumps? Nah, I'm goin' to the Marine Corps. But you were right about one thing—I'm getting out of this rearview town. Just got some . . . unfinished business to take care of first."

Eddie's blood went cold. "Look, man, I don't want no trouble—"

"And there *won't* be!" Trace said, still smiling. "Just tell me where I can find Forshaw—alone—and I'll let you go."

"I already told you, man, we ain't close no more. I don't know where he goes all the time."

"He walks Christie Cunningham home every day," Trace said casually.

Eddie froze. "How'd you know—"

"I've been suspended for weeks, genius. Plenty of time to watch. I know he walks her home from the bus. Mrs. Cunningham drives them off somewhere on Wednesdays, and takes *him* somewhere *without* Christie on Mondays and Thursdays. I wanna know where."

Eddie's throat went dry. "Listen, man. He and I

might not be close now, but he's still my friend. I ain't tellin' you nothin'!"

"Oh, you'll tell me," Trace said, his grin turning colder. "Because if you don't, me and the boys'll have a word with little Jonas."

Eddie's blood ran cold. "Don't you dare! If you touch him—"

"I know." Trace's voice dropped, soft and mocking. "Your poor mama couldn't cover the hospital bill. And it'd be your fault, Longshore. Now—it's Thursday. Where is Forshaw right now?"

Eddie gulped. "What're you gonna do to him?"

"That's up to him."

Then he remembered Zech's words on the bus. "Imagine Nation."

Trace's brow furrowed. "What?"

"Imagine Nation," Eddie repeated.

Trace's jaw clenched. "Don't play games with me, Longshore—"

"No, for real. That's the name—Imagine Nation."

Trace glared for what felt like an eternity. Then his eyes widened. "Wait—you mean that old bookstore on Plumbdale? Forshaw's going *there*?"

Eddie nodded, then added, "But not today. We got a group project—he's giving me the material. Try next Monday instead."

Trace narrowed his eyes, then grabbed Eddie's collar

and yanked him close. "No one's open on Veterans Day, you ignoramus!"

"Please, man, just don't hurt him too bad. Or too soon! We need this grade, man!"

Trace held him another long, agonizing moment, then shoved him back. "One week," he growled, then shoulder-checked him as he stormed off.

Eddie let out a shaky breath, knees weak, heart racing. Only when he was halfway home did the implications of what he'd done hit him. "What've I done?" he whispered. "What have I done?!" Cursing himself, he finally prayed—for the first time in years. "O God and Jesus, please forgive me. Keep him safe!"

* * *

"Well, Zech," Mike said as he handed over his wages, "it's been a week. How's the project coming along?"

"Great, actually! Surprisingly, everyone's been really involved. Christie had the genius idea to suggest we do something that Eddie enjoys."

Mike smiled. "She's always had a gift for reading people—bringing out their best."

"Amen to *that!* Though I still have to give Yeshua most of the credit."

"Don't we all? Still, you've been great influences on each other—she for your character, and you for her enthusiasm for reading Braille. She's excited about it now! You helped her finish the entire alphabet yesterday."

Zech flushed. "Well, I try."

"Honestly, I couldn't be more proud of you both."

"Thanks, Mr. Mike. That means a lot."

"Of course. And please, just call me Mike."

"Okay." He hesitated for a moment. "Hey, Mr. Str—I mean, Mike?"

"Yes, Zech?"

"Could you please pray for Eddie?"

"Sure! Why?"

"I dunno. He just seems . . . off lately. Won't look me in the eye. I just wanna make sure he's okay."

Mike's face grew serious. "Got it. I'll pray for him— and for *all of you.*"

"Thanks. Well, I should go. Mrs. Cunningham's busy, so I walked. Tell Mrs. Davis I hope she gets well soon."

"I will. Take care."

They parted ways, and Zech stepped outside to begin the long walk home. He had finished *The Stone of Ilamar* and loved it. He planned to buy a copy, as well as pay for the Bible that Mike had gifted him, and, once Christie learned enough Braille, the novel for her too. Money would be tight, but he hoped Rabbi Davis—Mrs. Davis' husband—would handle the repairs. The trick would be sneaking the work past his mom without her noticing the sounds or smells. For now, though, those were long-term goals.

In the meantime, his mind wandered back to Christie. She was like Charis to his Caleb, drawing out his best. Maybe he'd ask her to the Winter Formal on January 4—Louis

Braille's birthday, fittingly. But would she say yes? Or was that too much?

Suddenly, something slammed into his gut, knocking him flat. Rough hands dragged him into a dark alley, then yanked him upright. Wobbly and breathless, he ripped free, chest heaving.

"Who are you?" he said, his voice sharp like Caleb's. "What do you want?"

"Forshaw." Trace Seamore stepped out of the shadows, transformed—buzzed hair, sharp jaw, new muscle. The boyishly handsome karate master was no more. Before him stood a predator.

Zech knew what this was: payback.

"Trace," he said evenly. "What's this about?"

"Like I told Longshore—unfinished business." Then he rolled up his sleeves and took a fighting stance. "Go ahead, Forshaw. Take the first shot."

Zech gulped. But, he supposed, he was dead either way. So he feinted low, then swung high. Trace dodged and lunged, nearly dropping him. Zech sidestepped and turned to flee—only to find Trace's crew blocking both ends of the alley. Trace lunged again, slamming Zech's head against the pavement. Stars burst in his vision. He staggered up and threw a left hook—but Trace caught his arm and flung him down. Pain shot through his right shoulder as he landed hard. Then the others piled on, and soon his world became a blur of punches, kicks, curses, and sweat. Zech fought back, and thought he cracked someone's nose—but the odds were still against him.

Before long, he felt like a jellified puddle on the ground, unable to move.

Then Trace whistled, and his goons backed off. Then he straddled Zech, locked him into some sort of submission hold, and began raining blows all over—head, ribs, jaw, nose, and sternum. Zech didn't know it was possible to feel so much pain at once. Just as he thought he'd black out, Trace stopped and leaned over Zech's face.

"Feel like a mench now, Forshaw?" he hissed. "Still think you're some kind of hero?" Then he wrenched Zech's right shoulder and slammed his head into the pavement—hard—and he knew no more.

CHAPTER 15

REALIGNMENT

Zech came to in a white room with no memory of how he'd gotten there. A soft, steady beeping pulsed nearby. Machines, wires, and tubes surrounded him.

"Wha—Where am I?" he asked, his head swimming. He tried to sit up, but pain shot through his torso, and his right arm felt impossibly heavy. "What's going on? Why can't I move my arm?"

"Oh, you're awake!" A man in blue scrubs entered, relief in his voice. "You've been out for about two days. I'm glad I came in to check on you. How are you feeling?"

"Well . . . my head hurts, I'm sore all over, and no one's telling me what's happening!" Zech said, feeling woozier by the second.

The man—nurse or doctor, Zech couldn't tell—nodded knowingly. "That checks out. You're at least a *little* concussed."

"Concussed?" He searched his memory—and then, all at once, it came rushing back. "I got—pounded. Trace Seamore and six guys—not a fair fight. But why can't I move my arm?"

"Ah!" the doctor said, eyes crinkling. "That's good—you remember. That'll help the investigation. Unfortunately,

Trace Seamore skipped town the same day you were found. As for your arm: major shoulder dislocation, splinted. You also have an acute clavicular fracture, a bruised cheek and jaw bones, and several bruised and fractured ribs."

"Oh," Zech moaned. "Yeah, that tracks."

The doctor's eyes smiled again. "If what you say is true, you're lucky it wasn't worse. I'll go inform your family that you're awake."

He bustled out, leaving Zech to process. His brain still felt like jelly, but he glanced around. The splint jutted his arm out stiffly; an IV drip fed into his left arm. Questions crowded in: What had happened after Trace had knocked him out? Who had found him? And who *(or whom, as Mrs. Davis would have pointed out)* was coming now?

The doctor returned with his mother, Corban, and Olivia. At the sight of her youngest son, Joanna Forshaw burst into tears. *"Oy vey! Oy vey, oy vey, oy vey!"* she kept crying. Corban stood frozen, at a loss, as Olivia was busy comforting her future mother-in-law.

Finally, Corban stepped closer. "Does it hurt?"

Zech raised an eyebrow. "Does what hurt?"

Corban shook his head helplessly. "Any of it, I guess."

"Nah, just when I move—although now I've got the mother of all headaches. I dunno if *knowing* I have a concussion makes it worse—the gazebo effect or whatever—but I won't be sitting up anytime soon!"

Corban laughed shakily. "I think you mean the placebo effect. Pretty sure that's it."

"Yeah, that was it! I knew it ended in '*ebo.*'" Zech stole another glance at his mother, still sobbing into Olivia's shoulder. "Hey, big bro? Maybe make sure Mom doesn't completely wring herself dry. I'll be fine—might even take a nap."

Corban nodded. "Okay. Rest up, little bro. We love you."

"Love you too."

With that, Corban rejoined the women, and Zech closed his eyes and slipped off to sleep.

* * *

"You did *what?*"

"Look, I didn't wanna, but it was me or Jonas—and ain't no *way* I'm finna sell out my little brother!"

"So you sold out your best friend instead—to a *known* bully and black belt?"

"My mama can't afford what Trace would've done to us—literally!"

"And you think the Forshaws *can?*"

Zech groaned and opened his eyes. Two sharp gasps followed. "Guys?" he croaked. "What's going on?"

A curtain rustled, and Eddie and Christie emerged, looking sheepish. "Hey, buddy," Eddie said, his voice and smile strained.

"Are you okay?" Christie asked, her hands brushing the air in front of her. "Where are you?"

"Better now." His head felt clearer, though his arm and ribs throbbed. "You can walk her closer, Eddie."

Eddie hesitated, then guided Christie to Zech's right side, where his splinted arm jutted stiffly.

"Zech?" she asked.

"Right here." He smiled.

She lifted her hand, then faltered. "Can I—*may* I . . . see?"

"Sure, though I wouldn't touch my ribs right now. I'm not taking any chances."

Christie's dread was obvious, but she gingerly reached out, tracing his splinted arm. With a thrill of wonder, he noticed that she no longer wore her glasses—her beautiful eyes exposed for the world to see. Her hands froze at the splint.

"Does it hurt?" she whispered.

"Only a little, but not from you—just from Trace's last combo." He sensed tension. "So, what'd I miss? I was knocked out on Thursday and woke up two days later, right? Is that still today?"

"Yesterday," Christie corrected. "You fell asleep again after your family came. You'd been out fifty-one hours!"

"Oh!" Zech grinned. "You know, I know God commanded us Jews to rest on the Sabbath, but I don't think this was what He had in mind."

Christie giggled faintly, but the tension remained high.

"Hey, what's up, guys? Did something else happen?" His gaze shifted to Eddie, locking eyes with him. "Is Jonas okay?"

Eddie stiffened, then turned away. "You heard, didn't you?"

"Some. Mind starting from the top?"

Eddie fidgeted with his shirt hem, then faced him, shame etched on his face. "That day when we were grouped together for that project, Trace Seamore cornered me after I got off the bus. He'd been watching you, knew you went somewhere Mondays and Thursdays, and wanted to know where. Said he had unfinished business before he applied for the Marines. I tried to run interference—really, I did—but he threatened Jonas. I threw him off with Imagine Nation at first, but he figured it out. I told him Monday, tried to buy you time, begged him not to hurt you too badly, but one week later, he came for you. . . I'm sorry, man. I couldn't let him hurt my family. They're all I got, and all Mama's got."

A heavy hush fell over the room, broken only by the sounds of the machines. Zech took it all in, waiting for the anger to bubble inside him like boiling water. But it never came. Maybe he just lacked the energy, even though he was a little mad—or perhaps just disappointed—he knew Eddie. Despite their estrangement over the last few months, he believed him. And a passage surfaced in his mind: "Forgive us our debts, as we also have forgiven our debtors. . . For if you forgive others their transgressions, your heavenly Father will also forgive you. But if you do not forgive others, then your Father will not forgive your transgressions" (Matthew 6:12, 14–15). *How could he hold this against him when Yeshua had already done so much for him?*

"It's all right, Eddie," he said. "I forgive you."

Eddie and Christie both stared.

"I know what I was before—a sinner worthy of death.

But God sent His Son, Jesus the Messiah, to take the punishment for my sins, and He rose again to give eternal life. I've been forgiven. How could I not forgive him?"

Eddie blinked. "You're blowin' my mind, bro!"

Zech laughed—then winced at the pain in his ribs. "Talk to Mrs. Davis about it sometime. I'm sure Mr. Stroud or Reverend Presley can help you understand it better. In the meantime, pray and read a Bible if you can find one."

Eddie nodded, and then slipped out.

"Did he just leave?" Christie asked, raising her eyebrows—adorably.

"Looks like it."

"Well, I'll be fine. My mom's here; I can text her anytime."

"Point. Guess that VoiceOver thing really comes in handy."

Christie smiled faintly. "Siri, too, sometimes."

"Ha! I get that."

An awkward silence fell between them, and Christie breathed shallowly. Finally, she said, "Hey, Zech? I'm sorry. If I'd known what would happen, I would never have talked about Imagine Nation in front of him."

"No, no!" Zech laid his left hand gently over hers, resisting the urge to linger. "Christie, this isn't your fault! I was part of that conversation too. Besides, I bet if Trace was really watching us, he'd have found me sooner or later. He just chose sooner. Speaking of—have they caught him yet?"

"No, but they're looking. A detective may come to see

you. Trace's friends are already in custody—thanks to you. If he ever makes it to a Marine recruiting office, he won't be getting admitted with a warrant out for him." She squeezed his wrist. "Could you identify the people who attacked you in a lineup?"

Zech thought about it. "Maybe. But it was dark in that alley, and they swarmed me."

Christie paled. "Do you remember much of what happened?"

"Some. I remember walking home from Imagine Nation—your mom was at work, Mrs. Davis wasn't feeling well, and I wanted Mike free for her. They dragged me into the alley, and Trace started spitting threats. His guys blocked every way out; he slammed my head against the ground, then stepped back and let me recover—just to keep going. After a while, his crew took over, and when he finally whistled them off, he finished it himself. Yanked my shoulder, slammed my head again—and the next thing I knew, I was waking up here."

Christie shuddered. "Oh my goodness."

"Anyway—who found me?"

"A man cleaning the alley. He called 911."

"Then I owe him thanks."

She nodded. Then, softly, "But what about our project?"

Zech smirked. "Guess I'll be left-handed for a while."

"Are all your best notes in the Google Doc?"

"I think so."

"Good. At least Eddie can work with that. We'll just tweak some things here and there."

"Eddie knows how to keep things PG—I think."

Christie blushed. "All the same, we'll add creative touches, just in case."

"Fair enough. He's a good poet, but it's a group project."

Christie nodded, pulling out a silver metal thermos. "I brought something for you."

He sipped, eyes widening. "Is this your apple cider?"

"Yep! Mom says I've still got it, even if I can't see while making it."

"Well, it's perfect—especially after three days without taste."

She laughed, helping him set it aside. Then she clasped his hand, voice trembling. "Please get well soon, okay? I hate knowing you're like this."

"Don't worry. I'll be fine. Keep up the Braille lessons. You can catch me up when I'm out."

Christie smiled, shaky but sincere. "I'll visit you," she said, then got out her phone to voice-text her mom.

CHAPTER 16

PLANS AND PROPOSALS

Among the many tasks Zech had to learn to do left-handed—from eating to homework—one of the most annoying was that he couldn't wear his smartwatch on his left wrist and still use it, and he wasn't allowed to move his right arm enough to strap it on there either, even after the doctors let him switch to a sling. But soon he had an idea. About a week after coming home from the hospital, he asked his mom, "Could I please have my gaming system and games back?"

She raised her eyebrows. "You're not going to play on it instead of doing homework, are you?"

"No," he said truthfully. "Actually, I don't want to play with it at *all*. I wanna *sell* it and use the money for a phone and a *regular* watch."

His mother blinked, clearly blindsided. Finally, she said, "All right. I'm sure we can find someone who'd love a mint-condition virtual-reality station."

"And the games too. Maybe bundle them in for a bargain—the system plus extras. Oh, and could I please cash my earnings?"

"Why?"

He shrugged his good shoulder. "Call it preference."

By God's grace, it all worked out just in time for Black Friday. Soon Zech had about fifteen hundred dollars in cash. He bought a phone and a "dumb" watch, leaving him with four hundred fifty dollars, which he promptly added to his home-repair savings. With that, he went to Rabbi Davis after synagogue and asked, "Do you think you could do it for Christmas or something? I understand if that might not work."

Rabbi Davis frowned thoughtfully. Then he called his wife over, and they whispered quickly back and forth before she nodded.

"Do you know why Mrs. Davis has been under the weather lately?" the rabbi asked.

"No," Zech replied.

His rabbi nodded. "I think she was planning on telling you after break, but—we just found out that Ema's expecting our first child."

Zech's heart leapt. "Congratulations!"

"Thank you!" they both said.

"But you see, I want to be able to care for Ema during her pregnancy."

Ema stepped in with a smile. "But since you want this to be a surprise, I could invite your mom on a girls-only vacation around spring break—if you're well enough to take care of yourself by then."

"Sounds great! Thank you, Mrs. Davis, and you, too, Rabbi!"

* * *

When Christie came back from Thanksgiving break, three things lifted her spirits—and two weighed her down. The first development: Mrs. Davis announced grades for the group projects. Her group received a ninety-five—low for her, but remarkably high for her teammates. The second: Mrs. Davis announced she was expecting her first child the following summer. Just about everyone in English class cheered, and several girls squealed in excitement. Christie, however, raised a hand. "Will you finish the school year, or will you need a substitute?"

"I should be able to finish," Mrs. Davis said. "I may need a sub during doctor's appointments, but I'm hopeful nothing will interfere with my teaching." With that, she segued into *A Christmas Carol* by Charles Dickens.

The last development was bittersweet. Zech couldn't do most lifting while healing, so he and Christie began spending that period working on assignments—or catching him up on Braille.

"I know it'll just be your left hand for now," she told him, "but it's better than nothing."

Zech grinned. "True."

But her two shadows clung close. The first: her vision. Her right eye was now totally blind, and the left could see little more than light and shadow. While this *did* mean she no longer had to wear her glasses, it was little comfort when she could barely tell if the lights were on. Fortunately, she and her parents had found an orientation and mobility instructor who was teaching her cane work. She was regaining some independence—slowly, painfully, but surely.

The second shadow: a growing feeling she didn't understand—or perhaps didn't *want* to understand. After a week of wrestling with it, she finally sat down at dinner with her parents to talk about it over her dad's delicious salmon.

"Mom? Dad? There's something I need to talk to you about."

"Sure, honey," her dad said. Christie heard him set his silverware on the table. "What's up?"

Christie took a deep breath. "You know Zechariah Forshaw, right?"

"Sure!" Dad said warmly.

"Of course," Mom said. "What about him?"

"Well, I was just wondering if—maybe—I could take him to the Winter Formal—just as friends."

* * *

"So, Zech, what do you want for Christmaskah this year?"

Zech blushed at his mother's question. "You don't have to get me anything. I've already got my phone and my watch." He knew she couldn't afford much of anything else without it costing her dearly.

"Well, then think of it as a reward for all your hard work in school these last few months," she said. "So, beyond the usual socks, pajamas, and whatnot, is there anything in particular you'd like?"

"Well, he hesitated—"there was one thing I'd been

thinking about before I got injured, but I'm not sure I can do it now."

"Tell me."

"I *wanted* to ask Christie Cunningham to the Winter Formal—just as friends. But I'm not sure I *can* now."

* * *

"What would you do there?" her mother asked.

"Just hang out, I guess," Christie said with a shrug.

"So, you weren't planning on dancing?" her father pressed.

Christie winced. "I guess we wouldn't *have* to, now that you mention it."

* * *

"I guess that makes sense," Zech said—and hope flickered again in his chest.

His mother nodded, then asked, "Where would you go to dinner?"

* * *

"I think everyone's going to the Odessa Country Club," Christie said, remembering how people had raved about it. She hadn't cared at the time; she'd figured she would just stay home and study. "Is that okay? I'd be willing to cover anything if—"

"We can cover that, don't worry," Dad said, a smile in his voice.

* * *

"I can pay for anything that needs to be done," Zech said, wincing at the thought of draining his savings for the home repairs—but reminding himself that he could earn it back by working for Mike.

His mom nodded. "Very good. But what brought this on?"

* * *

"I don't know," Christie admitted, wincing at the half-truth. "It's just . . . ever since he became a believer and we started hanging out and studying together, I've seen a different side of him—one I don't think *he* even had before."

* * *

"Somehow," Zech said, "I see her in a completely different light."

* * *

"He's kind, funny, diligent, and forgiving," she said. "He's willing to do the right thing even when it's hard or costly."

* * *

"She's . . . pretty, smart, godly, hardworking—and . . . well . . . cute."

* * *

Christie tried to focus on Rabbi Davis' message, but her mind kept drifting back to Zechariah Forshaw, sitting nearby. Though she could no longer see him, she remembered his copper curls, the mischievous quirk of his smile, and the wry one-liners that always made her laugh.

For his part, Zech kept glancing over at Christie—her

short brown hair curled at the tips, the cute dimple in her cheek as she smiled about . . . something. *What was she thinking about?*

After the service, he found her and guided her outside. As soon as they stepped onto the driveway, he stopped. She stopped, too, waiting.

"Hey, Christie?" Zech asked, his throat tight. "There's something I've been meaning to ask you."

"Really?" she said, glancing over. "Because *I* wanted to ask you something too."

"Oh! Well, all right—you go first."

"No, it's fine—you go."

"Okay." He took a deep breath, his words turning to mist in the cold. *What am I doing?* "I know it might be a long shot, but . . ."

"Would you come with me to—"

"—the Winter Formal?" they blurted out at the same time.

Zech blinked. "Oh!"

She blushed. "Sorry. Were you—"

"No, it's—"

"Wait—"

"'Cuz I was gonna—"

They stopped and regrouped. "Sorry," they said together.

"Let's just start over," Christie suggested.

"Right. You go ahead."

"Oh! Well, all right." She cleared her throat. "I was wondering if you'd like to come with me to the Winter Formal—you know, just as friends."

Zech's heart leapt, sank, then soared again. "Believe it or not, I was gonna ask *you* the same thing!"

Christie let go of his arm, covering her face before he could see it.

"Like I said, probably a long shot, but I can pay for everything—"

"No!" Christie said, lowering her arms, her voice a little breathless. "My father said he'd cover it."

Zech wanted to pinch himself! *How was this happening?* "Are you sure?" he managed, trying not to croak.

"Absolutely!" She paused, then added, "We don't have to dance, you know. We can just—"

"Talk. Yeah, I was thinking the same thing—although Dr. Smith thinks I can take off my sling by New Year's."

"Oh, that's wonderful! But yeah—we can do whatever."

"Yeah." Despite the cold, Zech's face burned like a furnace. "So . . . we're doing this?"

"Yes!" Christie said, ecstatic. Zech was too.

CHAPTER 17

THE WINTER FORMAL

"Yo! You gotta be kiddin' me!"

Zech nearly jumped out of his skin, whipping his head around. "Eddie!" he gasped. "You want me to break my *neck* too?"

"Sorry, bro." Eddie fell in beside him as students streamed past. "I just heard you were asking Christie out to the formal."

"Asking her—what?" Zech's heart skipped a beat. "I'm not *asking her out* to the formal. I'm just . . . going with her. Wait—how'd *you* even know about that?"

Eddie shrugged. "Word gets around."

Zech seethed. "Who could've—" He stopped himself when he realized he was speaking aloud. "If someone was watching us—"

"Don't worry about it, bro!" Eddie clapped a reassuring hand on his good shoulder. "It was bound to get out sooner or later—that's just village life. And even if it didn't, people would've seen you two together at the dance anyway."

Zech blew out a huff. "Point."

"But seriously, I'm happy for you, man."

"Wait—for real?"

"Yeah! You two seem like a good match. Not sure I would've said that a couple of months ago, but—"

"Wait, wait, wait!" Zech held up his hand. "What do you mean, *a good match*?"

Eddie gave him a confused look, like Zech had just asked him to prove that two plus two equals four. "You know. You . . . click. You feel—oh, wait, that sounds wrong."

"What?"

"Well, I was *gonna* say you feel each other, but—"

"Yeah, good catch. But whatever you're trying to say, Eddie, just spit it out."

"I know, I know! Just tryin' to find the right word." He snapped his fingers. "Chemistry. Y'all got great chemistry."

Zech tilted his head. "You mean, like, romantic chemistry, or . . .?"

"If you wanted, I could see it." At Zech's sidelong look, he added, "I saw how you guys talked on the bus way back. She likes you, and you like her—"

"Wait—do you mean she *like likes* me, or just *regular* likes me?"

Eddie shrugged. "Okay, let me put it this way. If Trace Seamore came and put a gun to your head and asked if you thought Christie was romantically interested in me—"

"I'd say yes, but she don't wanna admit it—prob'ly don't even know *herself* yet."

Zech frowned. "Then he'd probably shoot you."

Eddie laughed. "Not before he asked what I was talkin' about—unlike *you.*"

"Okay, professor. Dazzle me."

"Don't need to. I think you can figure it out."

Zech cracked a half-sardonic smile. "What, not giving Trace as much credit as me?"

"Just tellin' you how I think he'd react."

Zech threw up his hand in mock surrender. "You're impossible."

"Listen, bro." Eddie put a hand back on his shoulder, and Zech lowered his own. "You're sharp with one-liners and even with schoolwork nowadays. But you *really* gotta work on readin' people."

"It's not that," Zech muttered, then blushed. "Okay, maybe a little. But believe me, it'd be *great* if Christie felt that way about me. But I'm just not sure she does."

"Well, how'd she react when you asked her out—sorry, when you asked her to *go with you?*"

"Well . . ." He recounted the whole charming, awkward interaction, and Eddie pressed him for every detail he could remember.

Then Eddie smirked, tapped his temple, and nodded. "Yep. I figured. She's got the hots for you, but she's in denial." He started walking off, then called over his shoulder, "And I'ma go out on a limb and say *you* are too!" And with that, he melted into the stream of students, leaving Zech's frustrated growl stuck in his throat.

* * *

"Thanks for taking me shopping for my dress!" Christie said, squeezing her father's arm.

"Anytime, sweetie," Dad said.

Just then, her mother came bustling back with an outfit for Christie to try on. "I think the colors and design of this dress would look great with his suit," she said.

"I agree," Dad said. "Let's try it on, hon!"

"What *is* his outfit?" Christie asked, raising an eyebrow.

"A white shirt, black pants, and a checkered tie with shades of red," Dad said.

"So what does *mine* look like?" she asked.

"Green, with white owl sleeves," Mom said. "You'll look wonderful in it. Come on! Let's try it on!"

Moments later—despite worrying she might look like a Christmas tree—Christie decided she'd get the dress. It fit perfectly: elegant, not too tight, not too loose. While her mom hunted for "a cute pair of shoes to match," Dad asked, "What's on your mind, sweet pea?"

"Me?" she asked.

"Yeah. You look like you've got something on your mind." When she stayed quiet—unusual for her—he softened. "Is it your friend, Zech?"

Hesitantly, Christie nodded. "I don't know what to do with these feelings."

"What kinds of feelings?"

She wrinkled her nose. "I don't know if I'm ready to talk about that."

"Gotcha. Have you been praying about it?"

Her head drooped. "I *could* pray more—and probably should."

"Well, then, I trust you to make the right decision—if you trust God to lead you—and remember what your mother and I have taught you."

Christie nodded. "Yes, sir."

* * *

Christmaskah dragged for Zech, though he barely remembered any details from that year's gathering. Corban and Olivia had helped him shop for his Winter Formal suit. He hadn't worn one since his *bar mitzvah,* and his old one no longer fit. Less welcome were the inflated alimony and child support payments that arrived instead of visits—a practice Zech found legally dubious at best, and one his mother detested.

He saw Christie at synagogue that Shabbat *and* at church the Sundays before and after Christmas. At synagogue, he helped her light a candle on Mrs. Davis' menorah.

After the New Year, the days felt endless, while hours raced by. Rabbi Davis moved the service to the morning to accommodate the Winter Formal, and Zech didn't see Christie in attendance. By the time four o'clock rolled around, Zech was both stiff in his clothes and anxious to see Christie. They'd agreed to meet at Imagine Nation for photos, but upon arrival, he didn't see her. Then, descending the stairs, Christie appeared. She wore a long emerald dress, white owl sleeves spreading like angel wings, her short hair immaculate. Zech's jaw dropped, and for a slow, still heartbeat, all he could think was: *Beautiful! She's beautiful!*

"Zech? Zech!" his mother hissed, then tapped him with a bouquet.

He jolted himself out of his reverie, blinked—caught off-guard—then took the flowers and approached her. *What should I say? My princess? No.*

Finally, standing near her father, clutching the bouquet as though it would protect him—Zech managed, "Hi!"

"Hey," Christie said, not moving.

Of course! She can't see the flowers! "I . . . I brought flowers," he said, holding out the bouquet and a rose corsage.

Her eyes widened. "Oh, thank you!" She let go of her father's arm and hesitantly extended her hand.

"Here," Zech said, walking forward a little so she could reach them. "A little farther—no, a bit to the right—there!"

"Mmm! What kind are they?"

"Irises. You know, winter flowers."

"They're wonderful. Thank you!"

"No problem."

Mrs. Cunningham smiled behind her. "Hello, Zech."

"Oh, hello, Dr. Cunningham, Mrs. Cunningham!"

"Hello there!" Dr. Cunningham said. "Nice suit, Zech."

"Thanks. Your daughter looks good too—I mean, you *all* look good!" Zech blushed.

Dr. Cunningham laughed. "No worries. We understand. So, you ready for a limo ride?"

Zech's stomach dropped. "Sure," he managed.

"Come on," Mrs. Cunningham said warmly. "Let's go take your pictures."

They did so, posing for photos in several different spots, including a few outside the storefront. Mike had set up the arch of Castle Ilamar, which made for an amazing backdrop, and he even came out to greet them. Then the long black limousine arrived, and everyone came out to see them off.

"Have a good time!" Mrs. Cunningham called after helping Christie into the limo.

"Have fun!" Dr. Cunningham said.

"Enjoy yourselves!" Mike called.

"*Mazel tov!*" Corban called, and Olivia and Zech's mom waved.

The limo door slid shut behind them, and Zech looked around, trying his best to take everything in. The interior was black leather, with a wraparound bench along the back and left side of the cabin. Then he heard a clicking noise and turned to see Christie folding up her cane. He laughed inwardly, surprised he hadn't recognized the familiar sound. Then his eyes were drawn back to Christie, who was already sitting on the side row, just where it turned the corner.

"No seat belts?" he asked.

"You don't need them," Christie said, patting the bench. "Here—sit down."

He hesitated, wanting to take her hand but refraining. *O Lord, help me!* "You've done this before?"

"Just once—for a second-cousin's wedding. All the bridesmaids arrived by limo."

"Oh. You look good."

"Thank you! So do you, I'm sure. And thanks again for the flowers!"

"You're welcome!" he said, his face flushing.

They sat in silence for a while. Finally, she asked, "So, how did you come to know Jesus?"

"Oh!" Zech hadn't expected the question. "Well, I started out at Beit-Aur Synagogue, which was Conservative—not quite Orthodox but not quite Reform, either. When my dad left, Mom started taking us to your godmother's place, and we all kinda absorbed Messianic Judaism without really believing in *Him*. My older brother Corban believed early on, but I didn't really care. We'd combine Christmas and Hanukkah whenever they overlapped, toss Yeshua's name into prayers, and read the New Testament at synagogue."

He paused, thinking of the previous fall, then continued. "But then, back in September, it felt like I was losing everything—my video games, my favorite class, even *Eddie* when I pushed him away! Then I started working for Mike and his Dark Room—and all his talk about imagination—really threw me off, and honestly, made me appreciate you more. I . . . well, I saw you at the grand reopening. While I was there, I found a Bible translation I hadn't seen before, and Mike actually gave it to me—free of charge! (I still fully intend to pay him back one of these days, no matter what he says.)

"Then, the next evening after *Shabbat*, I was reading the Haftarah—the portion from the Prophets—and it was Isaiah 53! Verses 4-6 hit me hard. Then I flipped to John 19 and 20 and—this is gonna sound crazy—I used my imagination, just sitting there in my room. I saw it. I heard it. And suddenly John 3:16 finally made sense: *I'm the one He came and bled and died for, to redeem me—a guy who'd treated Him as nothing more than the cream cheese on a bagel, just a garnish in my life, never actually giving my life to Him!*" He sighed. "Right then, I knew I was in trouble. I'd broken so many of God's *mitzvot*—His commandments. Then I remembered what Sha'ul of Tarsus— the Apostle Paul—said in *Romans* about believing in Jesus and confessing Him as Lord. But all I could manage was, 'Lord Jesus, I believe in You, I'm sorry.'"

He eyed Christie to make sure she followed. Her compassionate look told him he could continue. "And then—this might be the weirdest part, even after the whole imagination thing—everything *looked* different, especially the posters on my walls. You don't wanna know what they were, but let's just say that I hated them all in that moment. So I tore them all down! My walls were wrecked—reminders of things I'm ashamed of. That's why I'm working for Mike now—to save enough to get it all fixed. It's the least I can do after everything I put my mom through."

Christie's mouth hung open for a moment. Slowly, she nodded, then smiled. "Alleluia," she said softly.

"Amen," Zech said. He reached out and brushed her arm—then pulled his hand back quickly. "So how about *you?* How'd *you* come to know Yeshua?"

Just then, the limo slowed, and Zech spotted the country club entrance through the window.

"Are we there?" Christie asked.

"Yeah," Zech said, laughing at the timing. "Sorry."

"No, it's okay," Christie said with a smile. "I'll tell you inside."

* * *

"Okay," Zech said slowly from across the table, "I think we have a problem—I can't understand this thing, and you can't *read* it! I never thought I'd *rue the day* I chose Spanish over French."

Christie laughed. "Since when do *you* use phrases like *rue the day?*"

"Since I started hanging around people like you and Mike," he said—and she could hear the crooked smile in his voice.

Christie snorted, smothering it quickly in her napkin. *Oh, how she loved that invisible, cocky smile!*

"I think . . . I'll have the filet mignon," he said after a pause. "It's about the only thing on here I recognize. How about you? Want me to read anything to you?"

Christie thought for a moment. "I think I'll have the Cobb salad."

"Seriously? The one English item on here, and I miss it? And it's a *salad?*"

"It has more than just vegetables—chicken, bacon, egg—that kinda thing."

Zech paused, as though weighing his words. At last he said, "Fair enough. Any appetizers?"

"Garlic bread works."

"Got it."

After their waiter took their orders, Christie leaned back, taking in the Odessa Country Club. It was the official pre-dance dining spot, but thankfully quieter here than she would've expected the high school was going to be. Those who couldn't afford to eat here had other options—and the country club didn't mind, nor the restaurants cashing in on the flood of students, disgruntled employees or not.

"So what were you asking me earlier?" she asked.

"How you came to know Jesus as Lord," Zech said.

"Oh, right!" It had been a while since she'd told anyone, but the memories surfaced quickly.

"My dad came from a long line of Presbyterians, but he was more of a nominal believer until he was maybe sixteen or seventeen. He got saved at an evangelical vacation Bible school in Southern California—I think it was tied to some big-name evangelist. He went home and told his family, but they didn't quite get how serious he was. They figured that stuff like baptism as a baby, going to church, and taking communion—was enough. He graduated, went through college, and decided to become a doctor. He met my mom, who's from the Pruitt family around here. They're Anglo-Catholic, which are basically Anglicans who are more Catholic than Protestant. So they got married, settled here, and had me.

"I grew up going to Our Lord's Chapel, which is Baptist by doctrine and tradition. My parents let Ema Stroud—my babysitter—become my godmother when she was eighteen and I was eight. A year later, she took me to a camp in Indiana, where she was a counselor. That's where she and others explained the gospel to me: that I'm a sinner deserving judgment, but Jesus died for me and rose again, offering eternal life if I repented and trusted in Him. They baptized me in a river, and I told my parents all about it. My dad understood right away. My mom took longer, but she's happy about it now."

Zech whistled. "Wow. That's awesome! No wonder you and Mrs. Davis are so close!"

Christie nodded. "She's been a great mentor, even after she went to college and got married. Now that she's expecting, I hope I can return the favor."

Just then, their appetizers arrived. Zech helped her find the plate of garlic bread. She picked up a piece, blew on it, and bit into it—and found, to her delight, that it was just as good as she remembered.

"So, Zech," she said after swallowing, "do you know what you want to do after graduation?"

Zech went quiet for a moment. Presently, he said, "Honestly, I hadn't thought about it much. Back when I was obsessed with VR military campaigns, I toyed with the idea of joining the military, but I never really believed I'd do it. I just wanted to scrape through high school with the bare minimum requirements. But now that you mention it . . ."

"Zech?"

"Sorry, just thinking." He hesitated. "I guess I could keep working for Mike, maybe open another store like his. But lately I've seriously been considering becoming a teacher."

Christie nearly spat out her garlic bread. "A teacher?" she asked, trying to sound dignified. "You?"

"Yeah, weird, I know. But after spending time with you, Mike, Mrs. Davis—and even God, if I'm being honest—I think I'd enjoy passing on what I've been given."

Christie blinked, stunned. The old Zech wouldn't have cared one iota about life after graduation. But a *teacher?* "What kind of teacher?" she asked.

Zech snorted. "Now you *really* aren't gonna believe me!"

"Just say it!"

"English. Probably high school, since that's when I really started paying attention."

Now Christie couldn't help it—she threw her head back and laughed. "Okay," she said when she caught her breath. "Who are you, and what have you done with Zechariah Forshaw?"

"Me? Are we just gonna pretend *you* haven't rubbed off on me at all?"

She shook her head, unable to think of a comeback.

"So how about *you*, Christie Cunningham?" he asked, that cocky grin back in his voice. "What do *you* wanna do after May 2026?"

She should've expected the question, but hadn't let herself. Now she scrambled for an answer. At last, she sighed. "Well, to be candid, I don't really know." She could picture his cocked eyebrow—and hated it. "I know how that sounds, since I asked you first. But I've been so focused on excelling in high school that I figured I'd have senior year to decide. Foolish, I know, but . . ." She hesitated.

"But?" he prompted.

She hated how much she loved that smug tone!

"I thought . . . maybe teaching Braille wouldn't be so bad, since I'm learning it myself."

To her surprise, Zech didn't answer right away. Immediately panic hit her. Had he heard her? Did he think less of her? Was he crafting the perfect comeback?

"You know," he said at last, slow and smiling, "I think that suits you better than proofreading."

Relief washed over her. She even allowed herself to smile. "Makes more sense than *you* being a teacher."

"Ehh, give it time. You were born and *raised* that way. *I'll* grow into it."

She laughed. "True."

* * *

The common area of Odessa High looked like an ice palace—or as close to one as one could get. White streamers, balloons, sequins, and cotton balls covered everything. Each table—many of which had been pushed aside for the dance floor—held little electric candles that twinkled like snowflakes through the sea of white. Along the far wall stood a massive ice sculpture with a bin beneath it to catch the drips. Refreshment tables lined the edges, already drawing small lines of students. But the music? Three words: winter, Christmas, and *loud!*

"Here!" Zech half-shouted as he found a table tucked away from the nearest speaker, still close to the food but on the edge of the action. "You want anything?"

"Any what?" Christie yelled back.

"Food?"

"Oh—no thanks! Maybe later!"

Zech nodded, then kicked himself. "Fair enough."

For a while they sat and listened to the music, neither eager to shout over it. But eventually, Christie asked, "Do you like this kind of music?"

"Not at *this* volume!" Zech quipped.

"Granted! But the genre?"

"It's okay, though I prefer '80s rock. You?"

"I don't mind it. But classical's my go-to when I study."

"Seems legit. What about just for relaxation?"

"Classical, too, I guess, plus pop, hymns, maybe musicals."

"Cool!"

They kept at it a little longer before giving up, parched from the effort. Zech offered to grab water, and though Christie agreed, she insisted on coming with him. On their way back, Christie suddenly screamed, and Zech felt something cold soak his left leg.

"Oh my goodness!" Christie cried, mortified. "I tripped over something—either my dress or one of those stupid tablecloths. I'm sorry!"

"It's fine," Zech said, though his heart raced at the thought of anyone noticing. "I'll just towel off real quick." He sat her down with the cup he'd been holding for himself, then hustled into the nearest men's room to dab at his pants. *At least she can't see me. But everyone else can!*

After minimizing the damage, he grabbed another cup of water and returned. Glancing toward the dance floor, he spotted Eddie dancing with Audrey Manning—a tall blonde way out of his league. *Is that his date? If so, I'm impressed!*

"I'm back," Zech said as he sat.

"Sorry again," Christie said meekly. "Are you all right?"

"It's fine," he repeated. "Probably should've been watching where we were going."

"If it was my dress, then it wasn't your fault. Since I don't know, I'll operate on the assumption that it *was* my fault, just in case."

Zech considered this, then nodded. "Fair point." Then he grew serious. "Hey," he said, placing his hand over hers. "Everything I said earlier—about you rubbing off on me—I meant it."

Christie's brows rose. She sat quietly, then gave a small, resolute nod. "Could I tell you something?"

"Sure."

"I could say the same of you."

"Wait—me?"

"Yeah. You challenge me, you tease me—but I know it comes from a good place. And through it all, you push me to be better than I'd ever be on my own!"

"Whoa!" Zech let this sink in before answering. "Well, if you hadn't helped me with schoolwork early on, I'd be dead in the water—or *under* it, most likely. You slowed down to help a repentant bozo like me."

"But *you* did the same for *me* when I was too stubborn to learn Braille!"

Zech blinked. "Well," he said slowly, "Yeshua set us both the example."

"That's true!"

The words hung between them. Then a slower song came on, and couples started drifting onto the dance floor. And finally, the volume dropped to something conversational—perhaps even intimate. *O Lord Yeshua, be with me and guide my steps!* Zech prayed.

"Christie?" he said cautiously.

"Yes?"

"Why did you ask me to the Winter Formal? I mean, I know we're close, but why *me?*"

Her cheeks flushed crimson. "I've actually been wondering the same thing of *you.*"

Zech squirmed inside, then squared his shoulders. "You want the long answer or the short answer?"

"I think we've got time for either."

He drew a deep breath. "Well, honestly . . . I like you. A lot." Christie buried her face in her hands, blushing deeper. "I mean," he added quickly, "I couldn't see it at first. But the better I've gotten to know you as a friend, the more I've realized you're not just a bookworm with a pretty face. You're sweet, kind, smart, considerate, empathetic, funny, determined—and a fellow believer." He winced. "Do what you will with that, but I had to tell you."

When Christie finally lowered her hands, her eyes were puffy, mascara smudged with tears. Zech moaned. *I've ruined everything!* He handed her napkins, helping her dab without ruining her look further. After a long pause, she whispered, trembling, "Can I—*may* I—be completely candid?"

"Absolutely!"

"I . . . I like you too—a lot." Zech's stomach twisted. "I didn't want to admit it. I don't know when it started—maybe after you apologized, maybe after you saved me from Trace. But I know it grew when you offered to teach me Braille—blindfolded! I mean, who *does* that? And when you were in the hospital . . . I realized there might be *something*, though I wasn't quite ready to admit what it might have been. But why *wouldn't* I want something so precious, so beautiful?"

Zech thought for a moment, then ventured, "Maybe for the same reason you feared going blind, kinda like sighted people fearing the dark. It's not the thing itself, but the unknown that lurks within."

Christie's head snapped up toward him. "When did you get so . . . insightful?"

He shrugged. "Not sure."

They sat in silence as the slow music stretched on. Finally, Christie asked, "So . . . what do we do *now?*" *She was praying like crazy inside her head.*

Zech stood. "Wanna finish this dance?"

She almost protested—his arm, her blindness—but instead asked, "But what *are* we exactly?"

He sat again, taking her hand. "Christie Cunningham, will you be my girlfriend?"

She faltered, praying hard. *God, what do I do? God, what do I do?* At last, honesty won. "I'll probably need to check with my parents, but . . . yes. I *will* be your girlfriend, Zechariah Forshaw."

Zech exhaled, grinning. "Good. Let's do this."

It was awkward, even terrifying, at first, between her blindness and his injured arm. She doubted they'd make it as finalists in any dance competition. But for once, as the slow song swelled, Christie didn't care. Let the whole school stare, let them tease and whisper. Right now, this moment, this dance, was everything. They even braved the next more upbeat song—until Christie tripped and nearly fell *again*. Laughing, they retreated to their table, hands still clasped.

* * *

Parting at the end of the night wasn't easy, but they agreed to play it cool until they knew how their families would react. At eleven, Zech guided her out to the parking lot, where Dr. Cunningham and Corban were waiting. They exchanged thanks for the fun night, clasped hands, and shared a quick, chaste hug. Zech's heart fluttered even as it sank as he slid into the car.

"So," Corban asked as they pulled away, a sly smile tugging at his lips, "how'd it go?"

Zech hesitated, then grinned broadly. *"Hamzel haya tov,"* he said. *The luck was good.*

Corban's grin widened as he flashed a thumbs-up. "I*mma* figured you might try that. Congrats, little bro."

"It ain't over *yet,*" Zech said wryly. "She still has to ask *her* parents—and she's an only child." A thought struck him. "Wait. You think Mom'll be okay with this?"

Corban's expression softened. "You know her. She may not always show it, but I think she's proud of how much you've grown. She trusts you more now—to know what you want and to choose wisely. Well . . . more than *before,* anyway."

Zech smiled. "Thanks, bro. You're the best."

"Anytime. And for what it's worth, Olivia and I were rooting for you too."

"Really?"

"Yeah. We got to know the Cunninghams a little while you were in the hospital, and we love her too. Honestly, I think *Imma* does as well."

Zech chuckled. "Then I already know what she'll say in the morning."

"Yup. Short, sweet, and to the point."

"Pithy, more like!"

"H-Yeah, true." Then Corban sobered. "But really, I think it'll be just fine."

"Thanks, bro."

"Anytime."

* * *

"So," Dr. Cunningham asked as they pulled out of the parking lot, "how'd it go?"

"Good," Christie said, not sure how much to reveal.

He glanced at her under the glow of the interior lights. "Good?" he prompted.

"*Really* good!" she admitted, her walls lowering.

"Did you have fun?"

"Yes."

He let this sit a moment, then asked, "So, have you made a decision?"

Christie cringed inside. *He knows!* "Yes," she said softly. "I have—if you and Mom are okay with it."

Her dad reached over and squeezed her forearm. "You love him, don't you?"

Christie wilted. "He's changed *so much* since I first met him back at Odessa Middle! He's matured. He's kind, considerate, empathetic, selfless, courageous, fiercely loyal—he even gave me his water after I spilled mine! His testimony to Christ's work in his life is strong. And he sees beyond my limitations and pushes me to surpass them. *He's* the reason I started learning Braille."

"I like it," Dad said, a smile in his voice.

"And," she added breathlessly, "he's got plans. He wants to be—of all things—an English teacher, so he can pass on what he's learned from people like Mike and me! I just . . . can't believe it!"

Her father nodded. "Well, you know what's strictly off-limits until marriage."

"Yes, sir."

"All right. Then I'll leave the rest up to your consciences. Congratulations, sweetheart." He squeezed her arm again.

"Thank you!" Her heart soared—then quailed. "What about Mom?"

"I don't think she'll mind. I believe she likes him now."

Her heart leapt again. "Really?"

He chuckled. "It takes her a bit to come around to new guys, but yes—I think she's there."

Christie smiled. "Good, because I've been there a *really* long time."

CHAPTER 18

POLAR VORTEX

The blessings from Zech and Christie's mothers regarding their new romance seemed to fling wide the floodgates of village gossip. By the time Zech stepped into Odessa High School, whispers and pointing followed him down the halls. When he finally spotted Christie, her face was downcast and tense.

"Hey!" he called. "It's me—your favorite person!"

Her expression brightened instantly, then shifted into mock confusion. *"You're* not my Savior!" she teased.

"No, but I'm your *boyfriend,"* he replied, giving her hand a squeeze.

"True!" she said, smiling widely. "Very true!" Suddenly, she cocked her head. "Hey, do you hear that?"

"Hear what?" he asked, imitating her posture.

"That." She gestured with her cane toward the principal's office. "It sounds like a man yelling."

Zech strained his ears. Over the usual noise, he picked up the slurred, angry voice she'd described. "Well, *that* can't be good," he murmured. "I wonder what's going on."

"Probably none of our business," Christie said. "Besides, we don't wanna be late for class."

Just then, the principal's door slammed open, and a tall man with wild blond hair stormed out, face flushed purple. "I don' care what you or any hick police say—I ain't tellin' no one *nothin'* about Trace!" he spat, and his voice carried through the suddenly silent hall. "My boy's gonna be a U.S. Marine, and you'd better treat him with the respect that position deserves!"

"Deputy Gaines?" Mrs. Jenkins called, and the burly security guard approached.

"You touch me, you die!" the man growled, pivoting to face the deputy.

"Sir, you can either leave these premises without my help or with it," Deputy Gaines said evenly. "Your choice."

The man spat at the resource officer's feet. "With your assistance?! Like that Forshaw boy? He got what was comin' to him."

"Last warning, Mr. Seamore," the deputy said, resting his hand on his pistol. "Leave. Now."

A long, tense pause stretched. Zech's pulse pounded. Why was Trace Seamore's dad here, defending his son like this? Did Trace know? Had he put him up to it? The implications crashed over him. Finally, Mr. Seamore turned to leave, snarling. "I'll have your job for this, woman!" He swept the hallway with a glare that lingered, for the briefest moment, on Zech and Christie. Then he sauntered away down the hall.

"What was *that* all about?" Christie whispered, worry etched across her face.

"I dunno," Zech said, squeezing her hand. "But don't worry—I won't let anything happen to you. Not again."

"No, I won't let anything happen to *you* again!" she shot back, returning the squeeze even harder.

"What are you gonna do?" The words hit Zech the moment they left his mouth.

Christie's grip softened. "I don't know," she admitted, "but I *will find* a way!"

"I'll be fine, Christie," he said. "Why are you so worried about me?"

"Because his son put you in the hospital. What if his dad's worse?"

"Trace hurt you too. But he's gone. No need to worry!"

"So far as we *know*—which we *don't!* Besides, his dad was drunk on something. That's dangerous, Zech."

"I know, hon, but I can take care of myself."

"So you're saying I can't?"

"What? No! That's not what I—"

"Just because I'm blind, that makes me even *more* of a damsel in distress?"

He winced. "Look, honey, I'm sorry! I—I shouldn't've implied that. I just wanna keep you safe."

Christie exhaled slowly. "So do I. But I guess neither of us really knows how."

Zech considered this for a moment, then squeezed her hand for a third time. "Then let's figure it out—together."

She smiled and returned the pressure. "Right. Together."

* * *

By the end of the week, however, Zech was desperate. He'd asked everyone he could think of about self-defense training for Christie—including teachers, classmates, even Mike Stroud. Nothing. He'd started, naturally, by asking Coach Limbaugh, the lifting and wrestling coach, before strength and conditioning class that same day.

"Ah, Forshaw! How's your shoulder?" Coach had asked.

"Fine," Zech said. "Hey, could I ask a favor of you?"

"Sure, kid. What's up?"

"What do you know about self-defense? Do you think you could give Christie Cunningham some lessons? Nothing fancy, just the basics, enough to keep you alive if you're ever in a tight spot."

Coach's face turned pensive, then dubious. "I'm gonna be honest with you, kid," he said. "I really appreciate what you trying to do here. But training someone with *her* particular set of challenges is not my area of expertise."

Zech's heart sank. "Well, do you know anyone who can help?" he asked, feeling desperate.

Coach thought for a moment, then snapped his fingers. "You know who you *oughta* ask?"

"Who?"

"Deputy Gaines."

"Really?"

"Sure! He's got plenty of experience, and maybe even a secret weapon."

"Thanks, Coach! This really means a lot."

"No problem, buddy. Now hop on that bike."

Zech complied, excitement coursing through him.

But he did not see Deputy Gaines all that week. In the meantime, he kept looking. Online searches turned up dojos an hour away, which were useless. Hope was slipping. Then he spotted Deputy Gaines in the hall, and his heart leapt. This was his chance!

"Hey! Deputy Gaines!" he called, running up.

The officer turned to regard him. "Hello, Zech. What's up?"

"Could you . . ." Zech swallowed hard. "Could you please train Christie Cunningham in some basic self-defense?"

The deputy's brow furrowed. "Sorry, son. I can't do that."

Zech's heart dropped like a stone.

"But," the guard continued, "my wife can."

Zech blinked. "Wait—what?"

"My honey's a former Marine. And she's closer to Christie's size."

Zech couldn't believe his ears. "Will she agree to that?"

"Tell you what. I'll ask her this weekend and get back to you on Monday. Deal?"

Zech nodded. "Deal."

* * *

Christie, meanwhile, had been trying too—without much success. She frowned as she thought of Zech. He'd been searching diligently for leads since that Monday, but was losing both energy and hope—and very likely sleep—over it. Perhaps that's why he was late now: tracking down yet another dead end.

"Hey, Cunningham!" A sharp rap on the table made her jump.

"Hello? Who is this?"

"Just the most popular girl in Odessa High," a preppy voice said at her right shoulder.

Christie frowned. "Tracy Beaumont?"

"Nope. Try again, sweetie."

"Cora McClain?"

"Eww, no! One more guess, sweetheart!"

"Taylor Swift?" Christie said dryly.

Her mysterious visitor laughed. "Very funny! It's Audrey Manning!"

"Oh! You were Eddie Longshore's date, right?"

"Ugh, no! Please! I'm out of his league, and he knows it. I just humored him with a dance."

And he's probably fine with that, Christie thought.

"But *you're* dating that Forshaw boy, right?"

Christie tensed. "What's it to you if I *am?*" she asked.

"Whoa, whoa, whoa, girl friend. I'm just asking. No need to get testy!"

Christie processed this for a moment, then sighed. "Okay, yeah, I am. Why do *you* care?"

"Because I care about you!"

Christie rolled her eyes. "Right," she said dubiously.

"Really! The story's perfect: the jerk jock redeemed by

the blind genius, sacrificing himself to defend her honor, then sweeping her off her feet at the dance? Ahh! So cute!"

"Hold on," Christie said, raising a hand. "First, *I* didn't redeem him—God did. Second, he didn't sacrifice himself. He got jumped and concussed by a clutch of cowards in a side alley."

"A what?"

"Clutch. It's a term used to describe a batch of snake eggs."

"Oh!" Audrey said thoughtfully.

"Third, he didn't 'sweep me off my feet.' We were in love before the dance. I, for one, just hadn't worked up the nerve to admit it."

"Ooh!" Audrey said. "To him or to yourself?"

"Both."

"Eee!" Audrey squealed. "So romantic!"

Christie shrugged. "I mean, it works, I guess."

"Absolutely! But—"

Christie snorted.

"What?"

"You said *absolutely but* then immediately qualified it."

"Uhh! See, this is your problem right here, girl friend! You're leaning way too much into that nerdy, know-it-all vibe! Loosen up a little!"

"Why? Zech seems fine with it. And why's it any of your business anyway?"

"Because if you wanna become popular—like *moi*—"

She made a little kiss noise at herself. "—you need people to *like* you, so they'll *want* to be around you!"

"And what makes you think I *want* to be popular—*comme toi?*"

"Uh, because it's fun! Don't you want more friends than just your boyfriend? What if he leaves you? Who will you hang out with then?"

Christie's chest tightened. "He wouldn't leave me. Besides, no one else really gets me."

"Yeah—because they think you're a nerd!"

"*Zech* doesn't. No one really understands what it's like to *enjoy* reading, to *enjoy* learning, to work toward being your best."

"But that's just it! Don't you wanna have more friends to help you with things?"

"Would it be nice to have a few more friends? Maybe. But I've got Zech, my aid, Mrs. Davis, Mr. Stroud, my family—plenty of people who love, support, and at least *try* to understand me. And honestly, I'd rather have a few people who love and respect me than hangers-on who don't."

Audrey stamped her foot. "Fine! Be that way!" And she stormed off.

Then, from behind her, she heard the voice of the one for whom she'd been waiting. "Hey! Sorry I'm late. I was just talking to Deputy Gaines."

"It's fine!" Christie said with relief. "So?"

"Well, honey," Zech said dramatically, and Christie knew he was very pleased, "I think we might finally have a lead."

Christie's eyes widened. "Him?"

"His wife, maybe, if she says yes," Zech said. "But hey, progress is progress."

Christie tried to smile, but Audrey's words still lingered.

"Hey," Zech said softly, resting his hand on hers. "What's up? You look upset."

"Oh, it's nothing. Don't worry about it."

"No, it's not. Come on—tell me."

Christie sighed, then recounted the whole conversation. "She stormed off right before you showed up. But, dear," she said, gripping his hand tightly, "what if she's right? *Should* I try to make new friends, in case . . . you know?"

"Well, first of all, that won't happen, because I won't let it," Zech said, half-joking as he squeezed her hand. "But hey, if you want to make new friends, there's no harm in that."

"But what if there's no one else like me out there? What if she's right? What if I *do* push people away?"

"Honestly, you're probably asking the wrong guy," Zech admitted with a smile in his voice. "I don't exactly have a huge friend circle; I'm not the most socially aware, *and* I think you're perfect already."

"Oh, stop!" she said, giving his hand a playful squeeze.

"That said," he continued, "if it really bothers you, ask your folks or some adult you trust. I'd hate to give you bad advice. But Coach Limbaugh always says: don't take advice from someone you wouldn't take criticism from."

Despite herself, Christie smiled shakily. "Fair point, even if the grammar's off."

"Good truth with bad grammar, sweetheart!" Zech shot back, squeezing her hand again.

"That's funny, coming from someone who wants to teach English."

"Touché. Now, let's eat."

* * *

That weekend, a brutal wind barreled in from the west, chilling Odessa to its bones. Zech still went to synagogue and Christie to church, but everyone bundled up in hats and scarves. The weatherman warned of an incoming polar vortex—air so cold it would rival the Arctic. The city council scrambled, calling in snowplows from nearby towns and preparing to shut down schools and commerce, just in case.

But one man stayed busy regardless. On Saturday, Mr. and Mrs. Jenkins came home to find nails scattered across their driveway—clearly meant to puncture their tires. On Sunday, after church, a knife lay on their doorstep. The police were called, but the blade turned up no prints. And their troubles weren't over yet.

* * *

Zech woke to find his room freezing cold and his window rimmed with frost. The patched walls did little to keep out the cold. Dressing quickly, he shuffled to the kitchen, where a foot of snow pressed against the sliding glass door. Groaning at the thought of shoveling, he remembered that Corban had the family's only car, so maybe it wasn't necessary—since he lived away from home. With a shrug, he fried an egg, toasted a bagel, and texted Christie: "Hey, precious! It SNOWED last night—twelve inches, at least!" He sent a picture, then added, "Feel free to use your AI thing. It's crazy, but also kinda beautiful, like you."

Her reply came just as he flipped the egg: "Which part—crazy or beautiful?"

"Beautiful!" he texted back, realizing his faux pas.

"Are you sure?"

"Maybe," he wrote, along with a winky face.

She sent an eye-roll emoji followed by heart-eyes.

He copied the latter and sent it back, grinning. "Lord," he mused aloud, "what did I do to deserve such an awesome girlfriend?"

Just then, his mother emerged. Zech glanced at his egg and frowned when he saw it over hard. "Morning, *Imma*," he said, using the Hebrew term for "mother" the first time in ages. "How'd you sleep? I'd offer you an egg, but it's not over easy. Sorry."

She studied him a moment before replying, "Never mind. I'll make my own." Zech filled in the unspoken *thank-you* in his head.

"Snow looks pretty deep," he said, gesturing with his spatula. "Want me to shovel?"

After a pause, she nodded. "Sure. It'll be good for you."

Zech swallowed a sigh. "Yes, ma'am."

His mother's gaze lingered on him a beat longer, then she turned to making coffee. Briefly, he thought of cocoa, but knew better than to ask before proving himself with work. *Thank goodness this didn't happen on Shabbat!*

Twenty minutes later, he was bundled up in a hat, scarf, coat, boots, and snow pants from before his last growth spurt. The overalls wedged uncomfortably every time he bent with the shovel. "Remind me to add that to my birthday list!" he muttered.

No cars had yet packed the snow, which helped, but the flakes continued to fall, erasing his progress. Frustrated, he was about to quit when his phone buzzed. Balancing the shovel, he tugged off a glove and looked at a text from Christie.

"Hey!! You were right—the snow here's CRAZY!!! My dad's shoveling our driveway now, and the plows are finally making rounds. When we're done, would you like to come over and just hang out for a bit? Mom, Grandma, and I are making hot cocoa and cookies. And if you're behind on anything, we can work on that too!"

Zech snorted—of course she'd think about homework on a free snow day—but his heart soared. "Sure!!! I'm shoveling now, too, but my mom won't mind that . . . if the snow ever STOPS long enough for me to FINISH!!! SMH. But yes, I'd love to come over. Give me thirty minutes—sixty tops."

"Awesome!!! Can't wait!!!!!"

Zech pocketed the phone, smiling. "Thank You, Lord!" he whispered, then got back to work.

Nearly an hour later, the Cunninghams' front door scraped against the ice as it opened. The snow had stopped about forty-five minutes earlier, allowing Zech enough time to clear his driveway. The apple tree out front sagged beneath a snow-white cloak. The smell of baked goods wafted invitingly into the frigid air.

"Hello?" Christie called, her cheeks red from the cold. She wore a flour-dusted apron, fuzzy pink slippers, and thick white woolen socks.

"Hi!" Zech said, grinning at her.

"Hi!" she said, her face lighting up. "Come in!"

"Gladly!" Zech said, peeling off his coat and snow pants to reveal sweatpants beneath. "Wonder if I could've paid your dad to come over and help me—would've saved me some back pain."

Christie couldn't help but snicker. "True! But then I wouldn't have had an excuse to invite you here."

Zech imagined his mom's severe look and chuckled. "Fair enough," he said, then took her hand. "Smells amazing in here!"

Her smile widened. "Yup! Cookies and brownies. My grandma will dish some out for us; you can take some back with you if you'd like."

Zech's grin grew. "Sounds good!"

They walked into the kitchen together. A minute later, Christie's grandma appeared with samples of cookies and brownies, plus steaming mugs of fresh hot chocolate topped with marshmallows, plucked right from the bag. She wished them well and left the door open as she slipped out, leaving them alone.

"Mmm! These are amazing!" Zech said. "Did you make them yourself?"

"My mom and grandma helped," Christie admitted, "but it was my idea."

"Well, it was a great one. I can't tell if this feels more like Heaven, or if I'll just get there early when I die of diabetes from all this sugar and chocolate."

Christie laughed. "Consider it a foretaste."

"Heaven tastes like chocolate?"

She threw her head back in laughter, then took his free hand, tracing the lines of his palm. Though her left eye could barely see more than shapes and light, here and now *this*—*he*— was beautiful in a way she could understand—even if she still struggled to fathom it. Then his earlier remark reminded her of something.

"You know," she said, "I want to be able to make my own someday. Or at least more so than I can *now.*"

"Cool! How?"

"There's a training program for independent-living skills. I'm applying."

"Oh." Zech sounded a little disappointed. "When is it?"

"This summer—June, I think—in Missouri, so I'm not excited about all the outdoor O&M."

"How long is it?"

"Three weeks."

"Wow. That's long." The disappointment in his voice was plain now.

"Zech," Christie asked, turning toward him, "are you okay?"

"Me? Yeah, I'm fine," Zech said too quickly. He corrected himself: "No, I mean—I'm glad you're doing it. Really, I am. It's just . . . I'll miss you, ya know?"

"Hey!" She squeezed his hand. "It's gonna be okay. I'll text and call whenever I can. And when I get back, I can make us even more treats."

"It's just . . . what we have—it's all still so new . . ."

"It won't be by June. And I won't let anything happen to us. You have my word." She squeezed his hand again.

Zech let it sink in, then reciprocated the squeeze firmly. "Me neither, sweetheart."

Christie smiled, her other hand drifting to his forearm. She squeezed, then froze, pulled back, and straightened. "Sorry."

"Huh?"

"I should've asked."

"I was okay."

"No, I mean . . ." She hesitated, then resolved herself. "I think that we should talk about boundaries."

Zech blinked. "Okay. Did you have anything in mind?"

"My parents mostly left it up to us, barring the obvious."

"Right. The obvious." He chuckled. "No funny business."

Christie smothered a smile behind her hand. "Exactly."

"Gotcha. So what were you thinking?"

"We just need to be careful not to stray too close while still enjoying our time together."

"Okay. So what are you comfortable with—and not?"

Christie fidgeted with her hairpiece, silent for a long beat. Finally, she admitted, "I don't really know. I've never had a boyfriend before, and the only other person I had physical contact with besides family was my best friend Lisa, but she moved away when we were kids."

"So, you don't really know what you would and wouldn't like."

"No, not really. At this point, everything makes me nervous."

Zech pondered. "Okay. We can stick to hand-holding and hugs if that's best."

"That's just it. I *am* comfortable there, but . . ." She bit her lip. "I *want* to try other things—romantic things, like you read about in novels—but I'm still scared of taking things too far, too fast." Her words gushed out like a waterfall.

They sat in silence, processing and thinking. Finally, Zech asked, "You wanna try a tighter hug?"

Christie hesitated. *God, what should I do?* "I *want* to, but . . ." Suddenly, she made up her mind. "Yes."

"Yeah?"

"I wanna try it—but just a hug for now."

"Gotcha. How?"

"I'll stand—you come to me."

"Right."

She rose, tense, bracing for what she couldn't see coming. Then his left arm wrapped gently around her shoulder. "Sorry," he murmured, giving her a gentle squeeze. "Guess I forgot—the doc says I've got another three to seven weeks before this shoulder's back to normal. Prob'ly should've picked something else to try first."

"No, you're fine!" she said, quickly threading her arms beneath his and squeezing back as tightly as she dared. "I guess I forgot that too. This doesn't hurt you, does it?"

"No, it's okay!" Zech assured her, reaching around her other shoulder. "Once I'm healed, I'll give you a proper hug."

Christie smiled. "Just don't crush me. I've seen those biceps before."

"Oh, so you want a gun show, eh?" he teased.

"Oh, stop, or my family will kill you!"

"Hey, you said it first."

"Careful, hotshot. This house is *not* an open-carry zone—at least not for guests."

"Your dad likes to show off his biceps?"

"Uhh! You're impossible!"

He chuckled, then nestled his head on her shoulder. "You're incredible, honey."

"You're amazing," she murmured back.

"You're beautiful."

"You're cute."

He tensed in surprise. "Really?"

"I remember your face—your smirk, those copper curls." Her hands found them, smoothing, then playfully tousling them.

Zech snorted. "Imagine if your family walked in right now!"

"They don't have to. They can peek through the door."

He shuddered. "That a rule?"

"Yup! My parents have always been cautious about potential suitors."

Zech laughed nervously. "Fair enough."

"You're fine!" Christie laughed. "Just don't do anything—"

"Stupid?"

"Pretty much! I was trying to be polite."

"It's all right. I hope I never hurt you. I don't know what I've done to deserve a better girlfriend."

"Me neither!" She squeezed him tight.

"You said you never had a romantic partner before?"

"I *thought* I did once, but he was just leading me on. Have you?"

"I tried a few times, but *Imma* always shut it down if she thought it was a bad idea."

"*Imma?*"

"Means 'mom' in Hebrew or Aramaic—I think it's a loanword or something."

"Oh, nice!"

"You . . . like it?"

"Of course! It's sweet!"

"You're sweet."

"You're sweeter!"

"You know, I always thought it was cute when you raise your eyebrow."

Christie giggled. "I'm cute when I'm confused?"

"I dunno. It's just cute."

"Well, I always liked that cocky smirk you do when you're making fun of me."

"Making fun of you?!" He feigned offense. "You protest too much! I'm not making fun—I'm just having fun."

"By making fun of me."

"C'mon. You like it when I tease you."

"Only because it lets me tease you *back.*"

"Ooh, touché!"

Just then, a loud thump shook the front of the house.

"What the—" Zech started.

Then came a sound that froze their blood worse than the sub-Arctic gusts outside: a wailing siren.

"Goodness!" Zech cried.

"Mercy!" Christie cried. "Did someone spin out and wreck in the snow?"

Just then, Zech's phone buzzed. Pulling it from his pocket, he saw his mom's contact flashing, and he picked up instantly. "Hello?"

"Are you still at Christie's?" His mother's voice sounded tense and anxious.

"Yeah. Why?"

"Good. Stay there until either I, Corban, Olivia, or the police come by."

"The police? Mom, what's going on?"

"Someone drew a swastika in our front yard," Mom snapped.

Zech's heart stopped. For a long moment he couldn't speak. Finally he croaked, "Are *you* okay?"

"I'm in my bedroom. I've called the police, and I'm hiding out until they get here. You should too."

"Yes, *Imma. Shalom.*"

Before he could process the news, another call came in—this time from Eddie. "Hello?" Zech asked.

"Yo—can you believe it? Someone set Mrs. Jenkins' house on fire!"

"Whoa! *What?*"

Just then, the front door banged open, and Mrs. Cunningham's voice rang out, calling her husband's name. Zech and Christie sat frozen until the rest of her family entered. Her father carried the jagged top of a whiskey bottle; her mother clutched an opened envelope.

"Looks like someone hurled this at the door," Jeffrey Cunningham said, holding up the bottle. "And Molly found this on the porch."

With trembling hands, Mrs. Cunningham drew out a single sheet of paper and read:

Shoo that Jewish boy away,
Or go with him; receive his pay!

Signed,
THE KU KLUX KLAN

CHAPTER 19

GUARD'S HONOR

Long before the police were finished piecing things together, word had spread all over town. Theories about the Jenkins house fire ranged from a furnace accident to a flamethrower to a firework mishap. But while some argued one way and others another about who—or whom could have been responsible for the fire, the swastika, and the letter, two points were nearly universal. First, everyone agreed that Mr. Seamore—Trace's father—was the culprit of at least one crime, most likely the escalating threats against the Jenkins family, judging from what their children, grandchildren, and several Odessa High staff had said. Second, nearly everyone inferred that the local Klan chapter was behind the swastika and the threat to the Cunninghams, since their group was notorious for antisemitism and prejudice against the disabled. What people debated viciously was how, if at all, the pieces fit together. Some insisted it was a coincidence: After all, Ryan Seamore was already harassing poor Holley and Dale before the Klan got involved. Others insisted that it had to be connected: "After all, everyone knows Ryan runs with that crowd."

"But he can't be in three places at once!" the pro-coincidence people would counter.

"That's where the Klan comes in!" the pro-conspiracy camp shot back. "He set the fire to distract everyone while they did the rest."

"But why assume a connection at all? Both Ryan and the Klan had to know no one would be out that day!"

"Which is exactly why they planned it that way!"

And so the debates raged on—over dinner tables, video calls, and social media comment sections—all through the week, even as the village returned to school and work. Some whispered, "Could Trace have been involved? He hasn't been caught yet." Others, bitter and angry, muttered about the Jews' presence at all: "If they weren't here, those people would have something better to do than hating them!" Whenever a Jewish person was present for such talk, they would then leave in silence—fear, sorrow, or disgust written on their faces.

At school, every exterior entrance had a metal detector, and Mrs. Jenkins was nowhere to be seen. The assistant principal called an assembly, sharing what had happened as far as the police knew, and announced that Mrs. Jenkins would be on leave until the danger passed or the perpetrators were caught. But in hushed tones, many whispered that Ryan Seamore had scared her into quitting, just as he had intended.

Zech and Christie ate lunch in near silence. Every now and then, they squeezed each other's hands, sometimes wrapping their arms around each other's shoulders, but their words stayed locked behind their teeth, replaced by fervent prayer.

At last, Christie said softly, "I never should've applied to that training program."

"What?" Zech said. "Honey, no! What's that got to do with—"

"Because," she said, pain in every syllable, "if I leave—now or in June or whenever—I'll only be giving them what they want—including an open shot at you."

"That's not fair. You couldn't have known they'd do this!"

"But what if they try to hurt you while I'm gone?"

"But what if they hurt me *before* you leave, hon?" Immediately, he bit his tongue. "Sorry. I just mean—they're gonna do what they're gonna do. All we can do is prepare."

"But how?"

"Zechariah? Christie? May we sit down?"

They jumped, and Zech looked up sharply. Deputy Gaines stood across the table with a tall brunette in dress-blue BDUs. "Oh, sure," Zech said, pulse still quick.

"Thank you," Deputy Gaines said with a nod. "Honey," he said to the woman, "this is Zechariah Forshaw and Christie Cunningham—the young couple I told you about. Zech, Christie, this is my wife, Sergeant First Class Marie Gaines, U.S. Marine Corps, retired."

"Hello," Marie said, her smile warm but edged with quiet authority.

"Hello," they echoed.

"Thank you for your service," Christie added, rising to salute.

"It's been my honor." Marie's smile deepened, and she

glanced at her husband with amused fondness. "I like this one already."

For one of the few times Zech had ever seen, Deputy Gaines smiled. "I knew you would. They're good young people—both of 'em. And they need our help."

"I see." Marie's face turned grave again. "Richard filled me in on everything from the law enforcement side. I'm so sorry about what happened. I'm here to help however I can."

"Thank you," they said together.

"I've already arranged things with your parents," Deputy Gaines said. "You'll join us every Tuesday from three to five. Marie will work with Christie, and I'll work with Zech."

"Wait, *both* of us?" Zech asked.

"You were threatened, too, right?" Deputy Gaines leveled him with a look.

"Well . . . yeah. Fair enough, I guess. But my shoulder's still healing."

"No problem! We'll start with kicks."

Zech chuckled. "Touché. Count me in, sir."

"Great," Deputy Gaines said. "We'll pick you up after school and start today."

"And if there's anything else we can do for you two, just let us know," Marie added.

Zech was just opening his mouth to thank them when a sudden idea struck him. "Well," he said slowly, "there is *one* thing."

* * *

"Whoa!" Zech gave a low whistle. "Honey, they've got an entire gym set up in their pole barn."

"Wow." Christie wasn't as giddy as her boyfriend, but she was still impressed. *Looks like we're in good hands.*

"It's always good to stay in shape, active duty or not," Deputy Gaines said.

"True," Zech said as they crunched across the gravel. "You know, it's funny. While reading Mr. Stroud's latest book, I thought about fencing lessons. But something tells me this'll be a completely different beast."

"You can't always have a blade or a firearm on you," Marie said. "But if you can turn your *body* into a weapon, you can fight back in almost any situation."

"Yeah, wrestling's kinda the same way—although Coach Limbaugh warned us we could go to jail if we used our moves on the street," Zech added with a grin.

"That's why it's self-defense, not offense," Deputy Gaines said firmly. "The only—and I repeat, *only*—time when you launch a preemptive strike is if you truly believe you or someone you care about is in danger. Understand?"

"What if it's a stranger?" Zech asked. "Say you see some-one about to attack a stranger, but they don't even realize it?"

"Then alert the authorities," Marie said. "If appropri-ate, shout, distract, maybe scare them off. Physical intervention should be your very last resort—weapon or no weapon. Do you understand?"

"Yes, ma'am," Zech said after a pause.

"That said," Deputy Gaines continued as their voices

began to echo in the barn, "you're here to defend yourselves *and* each other, if necessary. What we've told you isn't just legal—it's a code of ethics. Guard's honor, we call it."

"We?" Christie asked.

"Richard and me," Marie explained. "Deputy Gaines has a little more legal lateral movement because of his position as a law enforcement officer, but being a Marine entails a similar commitment: to protect and serve the Constitution and the people of the United States. But a school resource officer can only do so much, and I'm just a consultant now, and you two have no rank or position whatsoever. We are *not* vigilantes, just ordinary citizens trying to survive."

"Got it," Zech said, then hastily added, "Ma'am!"

Marie chuckled. "I like this one, too, babe."

"Hard not to," Deputy Gaines said. As he spoke, a garage door clattered shut behind them. "Right. Let's start with stretches."

So they did. Marie guided Christie through the positions she couldn't quite grasp from verbal directions. To Christie's surprise, the first techniques weren't elaborate martial arts moves but brutal basics: kicks to the groin and hand strikes to the ears, eyes, nose, and throat. Zech worked left-handed for now, so they focused on legwork—mainly groin strikes. Each of them got a foam pad to practice on, and Christie was relieved she could brace against it as she struck. By the time their session was over, she felt dangerous—nervous about that—but also oddly strong, powerful, and confident.

"Great start," Marie said warmly. "I'm proud of your progress today, Christie. You're picking this up fast."

"Oh, thank you!" Christie said, blushing.

"Just think," Zech said as they headed back to the car, "if the worst happens, you could make sure there'll be no little Trace Seamores running around." He stomped on the gravel. "Bam! Gone without a trace."

Christie snorted. "Pun intended?"

"You know me." Mischief sparkled in his smirk.

"We'll review and build on this next week," Marie said, waving goodbye.

* * *

After Deputy Gaines dropped Christie off, Zech rode home with him to find his mother standing outside with a man in a black leather jacket, phone in hand.

"Oh, good, they're here," Deputy Gaines said as he parked and got out. "Howdy, Frank! How's it goin'?"

"A-okay, chief!" the other man called back, turning as Zech rounded the hood. "Just showing Ms. Forshaw how to pull up the security feed on her phone."

"Get everything hooked up?"

"Never better."

"Good copy." Deputy Gaines turned to Zech. "Francisco Gutierrez. He's an old military buddy o' mine who handles security consultations and installations. You asked for a security system—now you've got one. And Frank? This is

Zechariah Forshaw, the young man who so wisely asked for our assistance."

"Pleased to meetcha," Frank said, shaking Zech's hand. "And per Richie's request, it's on the house."

Zech's jaw dropped. "I—uh—thank you!" He wanted to hug someone.

His mother did, throwing her arms around Frank Gutierrez and breaking down in sobs. Deputy Gaines shot Zech a knowing nod and one of his rare smiles. "We'll talk to the Cunninghams too."

"They'll insist on paying," Zech warned with a half-smile.

"Let us handle that," Deputy Gaines said. "For now, rest up. We'll be back at it next week."

"Right. And thanks again!"

"Guard's honor, kid."

"Yes, sir. Guard's honor."

CHAPTER 20

FIRE AND WATER

"Cunningham?"

Christie traced her fingers over the Braille lines. For the first time in what felt like forever, she didn't have any research due, so she was free to do what she liked.

"Cunningham?"

Christie sighed. Maybe the library would've been better. She knew that voice—sharp, entitled.

"Not ignoring me, I hope, Cunningham!"

"I thought you were leaving me to my own devices," Christie said, turning to face her unwelcome visitor.

"Well, I *would* have," Audrey Manning replied, "except I happened by and noticed you sitting here all alone, with the Klan still at large—and your precious boyfriend nowhere in sight! How come?" Her tone dripped with fake sweetness, but the last question carried a jarring familiarity, as if they were old friends.

"I'm just reading," Christie said carefully, still gauging the situation.

"Oh." Audrey paused, then continued. "Anyway, I think we got off on the wrong foot the other week. Even if they act all high and mighty, I wouldn't want any *real* harm to befall any innocent student here. But honey"—her voice turned earnest—"you can't just sit here tempting fate like this!"

"What's wrong with where I'm sitting? It's my research period, and the library's too loud."

"It's not *where* you're sitting, darling! It's the fact that you're sitting here *alone,* unprotected . . . vulnerable."

To be fair, Christie saw her point—somewhat. She and Zech had only trained three times in two weeks. Still, she smiled sweetly and confidently—and perhaps laid it on a bit too thick—as she said, "I appreciate your concern, Audrey, but you needn't worry."

"Come again? Wait, 'needn't'?" Audrey blinked, confused—and oddly offended.

"I've been training," Christie said, her smile showing a bit more pride than she felt she deserved.

"Training? How? By whom?"

Christie couldn't help but be amused by Audrey's suddenly proper use of grammar. "A former Marine and her husband."

Audrey went quiet for a long moment. Finally, she said, "So if a Klansman snuck up behind you right now—"

"Deputy Gaines would've had him cuffed before he got the chance."

Audrey spluttered, then rallied, "All right, but say they did—snuck up and put you in a chokehold, maybe."

And there goes the good grammar. "Then I'd scream like a banshee and claw his eyes out, welcome him into the club."

"The club?"

"The blind and visually impaired community."

"Oh. . . . But what if—"

"Oh, hey, Christie! Hi, Audrey!"

Christie's heart leapt. *Thank God!* "Hi, Zech!" she called a little louder than usual, savoring the likely expression on Audrey's face. "What's up?"

"Oh, nothin' much." Zech strolled over. "Today was cardio, but all the bikes were taken, and my rehab trainer's out, so Coach let me go early. What're *you* up to?"

"Not much either. I was practicing my Braille exercises. Then, I was explaining to Audrey how I'd escape if a Klansman tried to strangle me."

"Oh. Did you tell her about the whole gouging-out-the-eyes thing?"

"Mhm!"

"Good stuff!"

"Okay!" Audrey snapped. "This is cute and all, but Forshaw—you won't always be around. And *you,* Cunningham—what if he doesn't *want* to be? Why make this so difficult for the rest of us?"

Silence fell heavily between them.

"Who hurt you?" Zech asked, pity and confusion edging his tone.

Audrey recoiled as if slapped. Then, with a squeal of rubber, she spun on her heel. "Don't say I didn't warn you if something bad happens!" she called, disappearing down the hall.

"What was *that* about?" Christie asked, brow raised.

"Not sure," Zech said, "but I'd like to find out."

"If nothing else, we should pray for her," Christie said.

"True. Still, I don't quite like the sound of that *last* bit."

"I can't say that I blame you for worrying, dear."

Zech sat beside her, placing a hand on hers. "So, how's your practicing coming?"

"It was going well—before *she* showed up." Christie chuckled. "But it's fine."

"I was surprised, honestly. No research due?"

"Nothing pressing. I'm all caught up—even ahead for the moment!" Christie said.

"Whoa. Congrats, honey!"

"Thanks!"

They held hands for a minute. Then Zech said, "I just realized—our one-month anniversary's next Tuesday."

"It is!" Christie squeezed his hand, beaming. "I can't believe it! And a month after that, *you'll be turning eighteen!*"

"Yeah! Kinda nerve-racking, not gonna lie. And God willing, my shoulder should be fully healed by then."

"Yay! How will you know?"

"I've got an appointment tomorrow at eight. Will you be okay getting to class without me?"

"Yes, I'll be all right. That's exciting, though! I'll be praying for you."

"Thanks." He sighed. "I can't believe how much has changed since . . ."

"Since when, dear?"

"I dunno. For sure since last September. Honestly, in

a strange way, if my mom hadn't taken my gaming station, I might never have found Imagine Nation, fallen in love with you, or had my world rocked enough to accept Messiah."

"I think it would've happened eventually, just maybe not in the same way. Although sometimes I wonder how things would've gone if Miss Ema hadn't invited me to that summer camp." Suddenly, a thought struck her. "Hey, hon?"

"Yeah?"

"Have you ever thought about getting baptized?"

Zech hesitated. "I'm not sure. I've been so busy and haven't thought much about it. But . . . I dunno. Is that even a thing Jewish believers do?"

"It's a *Christian* thing."

"Yeah, but I thought maybe Gentile Christians did that, and Jewish believers did something else."

"Nope. Jesus was baptized, and so were all the early believers—all Jewish."

"Oh. I hadn't thought that through."

"Hasn't anyone ever gone public with their faith at Miss Ema's place?"

"Yeah, but we call it immersion—like a *mikvah,* a ceremonial bath."

"Same thing."

"Wait, really?"

"Yep. It's like saying *Messiah* or *Christ or Anointed One*—all different words, same meaning."

"Oh! Then what've I been waiting for? I'll tell Rabbi Davis. You can come if you want."

"Of course!"

"Thanks, hon. I needed that."

"Anytime, dear!"

* * *

"Thanks again, bro!" Zech called as he hopped out of the car into the drop-off lane.

"No prob, little bro," Corban said with a grin. "Congrats on the clean bill of health. Just try not to get beat up again, okay?"

"No promises!"

Corban shook his head, but Zech caught the smile in his eyes even as he tried to hide it. "Well, see ya later! *Shalom!*"

"*Shalom!*"

With a spring in his step, Zech mounted the curb and started toward the athletic wing. The door closest to the drop-off lane was automatically locked without a specially authorized student badge, which Zech did not have. The main office sat on the other side of the building and had an intercom for admittance. But to get there, one had to loop around the end of the school, and the academic wing which split into a Y shape. So, most students chose to go around the athletic wing on the other end. As he neared the corner, he stuffed his fists into his coat pockets against the cold. He found himself wishing he could see the security guards posted around the school. He knew that they were trained to blend in, but he felt better when he could see them. *God protect me, and keep Christie safe.*

Just then, a flicker of movement caught his eye—someone slinking along the side of the building. The shadow moved in step with him. Zech's blood ran cold, and a gust rattled the bare branches ahead like dead men's bones. Zech slowed his stride, heel to toe, glancing in all directions. The shadow didn't break pace. Maybe it hadn't seen him.

Then another figure emerged, following and pacing the first, moving just as stealthily. Zech's pulse spiked. When all three stepped into the light at once, Zech gasped softly between his teeth. Both men wore camouflage, faces streaked with grease paint. The first was large, his disguise failing to mask the flush on his cheeks. Zech saw him clutching two cylindrical containers: a spray paint can and a glass bottle rag-stuffed at the top. Zech recognized Ryan Seamore, and from countless video games, he recognized the weapon: a Molotov cocktail. But it was the second figure that rooted Zech to the spot: tall, slender, hair shaved in an arrow shape, and clutching a pistol. Zech recognized Gavin Trace Seamore.

Immediately his heart and thoughts raced. What were they doing here? Were they working together? What should he do? Then Deputy Gaines' voice echoed in his head: Don't panic. Think. Take a breath, look around, make a call.

So he did. Breathing steadily, he followed the Seamores discreetly and studied their movements. The pair stalked in the shadow of the building with the precision of hunters. Then, to his horror, Trace raised his gun! Zech's heart hammered against his ribs. Was Trace really about to shoot up the school? *Why?* And what should he—could he—do about it?

He glanced around. No security in sight. Two hostiles. An open parking lot sat ahead to his right. Down a sidewalk to his left, the door to the boys' locker room was propped open an inch. Immediately Zech remembered the fire alarm on the wall of the locker room. But was that legal? Marie Gaines' words came back to him: We are not vigilantes, just ordinary citizens trying to survive.

He knew what he had to do. Turning on the spot, Zech darted inside, skidded to a halt, then pulled the alarm.

The effects were immediate. The alarm began blaring loudly throughout the school. Quickly he turned and fled back outside, just in time to see Deputy Gaines burst through the door at the far end of the sidewalk.

"He's got a gun!" Zech shouted, pointing to Trace. "And he's got a Molotov!" he said, pointing to Ryan.

At the sound of Zech's voice, Ryan Seamore whirled, and immediately saw the danger. With a snarl, he hurled the spray can and the bottle, both landing harmlessly in the grass, then bolted for the nearby parking lot.

Zech's panic was climbing again when a sharp command split the autumn air. "Freeze!" To Zech's amazement and joy, three more armed security guards joined Deputy Gaines, and they surrounded Ryan just as he reached the center of the empty lot, cuffing him. One of them, a short Hispanic man, began hunting for the can and bottle.

Trace, however, was not so easily cowed. He fired wildly at Gaines, but in his fury all his shots went wide. When he ran out, he threw his gun down and charged. The fight that followed astounded Zech. He knew both were good, but he'd never seen Deputy Gaines in full combat mode. In the end, Gaines kicked Trace in the kidney, sending him sprawling, then trained his gun on him as one of the men guarding Ryan came over and cuffed the younger Seamore.

"Zech!" Gaines called, sprinting over. "Are you all right?"

"I'm okay," Zech said, heart pounding. "But Ryan Seamore's Molotov—"

"Torres is looking for it. He threw it but luckily it landed in the grass and didn't break open."

"Sir," Zech said nervously. "I pulled the fire alarm. Was that wrong?"

"No Zech, not in an emergency situation," Gaines said. "You did the right thing young man."

Zech nodded, then smiled. "Guard's honor."

"Guard's honor," Gaines said, smiling proudly.

* * *

"Say that again?" Christie's heart hammered in her chest as she processed her boyfriend's words.

"I think I just saved the school from a Seamore family hate crime."

Her eyes flew wide. "*Both* of them?"

"Yeah. Can't quite believe it myself."

"And you totally play it off saying, 'Hey, hon, sorry I'm late'?!"

"Didn't wanna spill the beans on something like that in front of the whole class."

"And I get that. But Zech! That's . . . this is—"

"Crazy? Yeah."

She inhaled and exhaled quickly, then steadied herself. "Okay, spill."

Zech recounted everything. By the end, Christie's eyes were saucers. Silence stretched—thirty seconds that felt like an eternity.

"Zech," she whispered, "you're a hero." Then joy flooded her, and a delighted laugh escaped her. "You're an actual hero!" Without thinking, she stood up, threw her arms around him, and kissed him hard. True, it ended up on the cheek, not the lips, but she squeezed him tight—then remembered where they were. Pulling back, flustered, she stammered, "Sorry. PDA."

Zech didn't answer for a moment, and Christie panicked. Surely, if she had ever overstepped, it was now! Then, to her astonishment, he pulled her in, turned her face tenderly to the side, and kissed her on the cheek.

"Zech!" she cried, mortified.

He broke away, and she felt him shrug. "You started it, hon," he said, and she could sense that cocky grin she loved so much.

To her annoyance, she couldn't think of a comeback.

"But honestly," he continued, "I don't feel like much of a hero. Love your neighbor as yourself, and all that. Deputy Gaines and his guys were way cooler than me, trust me."

"Still . . . I can't believe you, Zech."

"Whaddaya mean?" he asked, sounding nervous.

"I mean . . . you've changed so much since sixth grade. You used to not to care about anyone but yourself, and now you save the entire school from arson and a hate crime?! Who are you, and what have you done with Zechariah Forshaw?!"

"Me? Oh, I couldn't have done that. But God can change people like that."

"Zech?" Christie squeezed his hand.

"Yeah?"

"You are seriously tempting me to break school rules and kiss you right here, right now, on that smart, godly mouth of yours!"

Zech snickered, a little rattled but clearly pleased. "If you wait till after school, I'll oblige you."

Christie beamed. "Deal. Though . . . maybe not in public just yet."

"Didn't stop you just *now.*"

"Oh, stop! That was in the heat of the moment, and you know it!"

"Touché. No worries, hon." He squeezed her hand lovingly. "We'll figure it out—together."

"Absolutely. Together."

* * *

Forshaw,

    You were right. Please tell Christie. I'm sorry.

Audrey

CHAPTER 21

FULL IMMERSION

Joanna Forshaw hadn't laughed so hard—or so much—in ages! She and Ema had been on vacation for the past week, and now they sat laughing like old friends as Jonathan Davis drove them from the airport.

"So, how was the trip?" Jonathan asked.

"Perfect," Ema said from the passenger seat, grinning.

"Wonderful," Joanna admitted. "I hadn't realized how much I needed it until I was right in the middle of it—although I *am* disappointed I missed Zechariah's eighteenth two days ago."

"No worries," Jonathan said with a smile. "I can assure you that he missed you too. But you'll come by for synagogue?"

"Yes, of course, but . . ."

"Go on," Ema urged.

"It's just . . . I want to see Zechariah again, make sure he's safe," Joanna said.

"Joanna, I told you," Ema reminded her. "The Seamores' testimony was enough to bring in the state police and round up the whole Klan chapter. And yours and the Cunninghams' places are locked up tighter than Fort Knox! They'll be fine."

"And if it helps," Jonathan added, "Zech will be at our place when we get there. He's been looking forward to seeing you. It's going to be a very special service."

Joanna's eyes widened. "Is he performing *aliyah?*" she asked, her heart swelling with pride at the thought of her boy standing before the congregation, reading from the sacred Torah scroll.

"You'll have to come and see," Ema said with a wink.

"But I'm not wearing my *Shabbat* best."

"Neither am I. It'll be all right."

"You're pregnant. You have an excuse."

"Just trust us. It's gonna be just fine."

Joanna sighed. "All right."

She spent the rest of the ride taming her hair and wondering what awaited her at the Davis home. When they arrived, she noticed a line of cars stretching down the block, forcing them to park on the street and walk. When they got there, she was startled to see a much larger crowd than usual—some of them Gentiles, including Michael Stroud from Imagine Nation. She frowned. *What was going on?*

"Sorry about the wait, brothers and sisters," Jonathan said as he unlocked the door.

No one seemed to mind, and soon everyone filed in. Joanna moved to take her usual seat—then stopped. In the center of the living room stood a free-standing tub. *Someone's doing a mikvah today?* Then her heart leapt. *Could it be . . .?*

These thoughts consumed her as prayers began. Dimly, she noticed the Cunninghams out of the corner of her eye, but her attention fixed upon the tub as Zechariah stepped forward. He stood behind the tub in a T-shirt and shorts, nervous but resolved.

"Zechariah ben Pinchas," Rabbi Davis said solemnly, laying a hand on his head. "We gather today to witness your immersion into *Yeshua Hamashiach*, identifying yourself with His death, burial, and resurrection. What reason do you give for taking this step?"

Zech drew a deep breath, glancing around at his mother, Corban, Christie, Ema, and Mike. "By God's grace, I am what I am," he began, nerves aflutter. "But I know what I once was: a liar, a thief, a blasphemer, an adulterer at heart, insolent, angry, and disobedient to parents. Yet in the words of Emissary Sha'ul of Tarsus—known to most as the Apostle Paul—'It is a trustworthy saying and deserving full acceptance: that Christ [Messiah] Jesus came into the world to save sinners, among whom I am foremost' (1 Timothy 1:15). But He chose me in Himself to be an example for all who would believe in His name, that He died on the tree to make atonement for sins as the perfect Passover Lamb in accordance with our Scriptures, was buried, and rose again the third day in accordance with our Scriptures—so that believing in Him, you may not perish but dwell with Him forever as His prized possession, and He be your God forevermore." Then, in Hebrew, he added: "Blessed are You, Lord God, King of Heaven and Earth, for this gift of atonement and salvation."

Joanna blinked back tears as the room erupted in applause. Rabbi Davis helped Zech into the tub. "Zechariah ben Pinchas, do you confess with your mouth that Yeshua is Lord, and believe in your heart that God raised Him from the dead?" he asked.

"Yes."

"Then it is my privilege to immerse you as a brother in the name of the Father, the Son, and the Holy Spirit: *Ba hashem HaAv, HaBen, v'HaRuach Hakodesh.*"

Joanna's tears escaped her eyes as her son went under, then reemerged to thunderous applause. Corban slapped his little brother heartily on the back. Mike caught his eye, nodding and smiling. Jeffrey Cunningham gave him two thumbs up. Before the crowd could rush him, Rabbi Davis wrapped Zech in a towel and whisked him away. But Joanna was still lost in her thoughts. *Was this what had changed her boy so profoundly? Was Yeshua more than a cultural novelty or the symbol of her community?* Now she thought she understood what Corban had seen years ago. *This Yeshua—He was real.*

Just then, a gentle arm slipped around her shoulders. She looked up to see Ema Davis smiling knowingly. "You see it now, don't you?" she asked softly.

Joanna managed a shaky nod. "He is real," she choked out. "And He's changed my son."

"He saved what you feared was lost forever. Only the Good Shepherd can bring the lost sheep home," Ema said, squeezing her shoulders warmly.

At this, Joanna broke down completely. "I believe," she sobbed, "or at least, I *want* to believe. My heart's been hard for so long—bitterness, anger, unforgiveness, trained in self-discipline but thirsting for compassion. But is it too late for me?"

"Never!" Ema's voice was a low, excited thrum in her ear. She held Joanna close and prayed with her.

* * *

Later, Rabbi Davis drove the women to Joanna's house, carrying her luggage inside himself. Just then, Corban arrived with Olivia, Zech, and Christie in tow.

"Hey, *Imma?*" Zech asked nervously. "I've got something to show you."

"You want to break my heart twice in one day?" she asked before she could stop herself.

"Not intentionally!" Zech protested, smiling awkwardly. "Actually, I was hoping for the opposite. Rabbi Davis and I have been working on something for a while now."

She arched an eyebrow, but shrugged. "All right. Show me."

Zech nodded, punched in the security code, and led them into the foyer, then opened the door to his room. It had once been scarred and battered, but now it was pristine—walls smooth and painted cream, blackout curtains drawn, and the Ten Commandments plaque hanging above the bed. The floor gleamed with wood planking that stretched into the hall. As her eyes followed it, she traced the wood around the room and out the door. Heart racing, she darted into the hallway. Sure enough, the entire first floor had been redone—new flooring, fresh paint, and spotless rooms, even new carpet on the stairs and the second floor.

She couldn't contain it. She screamed—then burst into tears.

"When? How? Why?" she cried, overwhelmed.

Zech wrapped her in his strong arms. "I just wanted to make things right," he said softly.

"All that saving?" she sniffed.

Zech nodded. "Originally, I wanted to just do my room, but Rabbi Davis, Deputy Gaines, and Mr. Cunningham helped arrange a full remodel. Corban helped plan what you've always wanted. I hope it measures up."

"Measures up?!" Joanna was speechless. Then—something she rarely did anymore—she smiled—and that said it all.

* * *

That night, Joanna sat alone in the living room. Both her boys were out on a double date with their respective ladies—her future daughters-in-law, she thought to herself—and she lingered at home, deep in thought. Could she do this? *Should* she?

Well, she thought, *at least I can try.*

Taking a deep breath, she dialed a number she hadn't called in years. It rang and rang. Just as she was about to give up, a tired voice answered, "Hello?"

"Darren?" she said, surprised by the nervousness in her own voice.

"Joanna . . . Somethin' wrong? My last payment not go through?"

"No, no—it's not that!" She felt like an awkward teenager again.

"Well, what is it? Jessa's making dinner, and Rivkah needs help with her homework."

To her surprise, it was not anger or bitterness that welled up within her, but only sorrow. "I . . . I just wanted to tell you something."

Darren Forshaw was quiet for a long, agonizing moment. Finally, he said, "Go on."

She steadied herself. "I forgive you, Darren."

Silence.

"I know things can never go back to how they were, and I don't want them to. I just wanted to tell you that I forgive you."

Another pause. "Why are you telling me this?"

"Because," Joanna said gently, "your sons and I all believe in Yeshua."

The silence felt deafening, and Joanna feared how he was receiving her words. "I know what you're thinking—Jews don't believe in Jesus—but . . . well, we do. I don't expect you to understand or approve, but I thought you deserved to know."

Darren was silent for a moment longer, then said, "I . . . see." Another pause, then: "Good for you." Then the line went dead.

"Well," she whispered, half to herself, "at least I told him." She looked up to Heaven and lifted her hands. "Blessed are You, Lord God, King of Heaven and Earth, that You have given us this life, this forgiveness, and this grace. Amen."

EPILOGUE
GRADUATION DAY

May 23 dawned warm, clear, and blue over the Odessa High School football stadium. A soft spring breeze nudged fluffy cumulus clouds across the sky. Up above, the bleachers buzzed with conversation—the whole town seemed to have shown up. Down on the field, the class of 2026 braced for hours of pomp and circumstance before reuniting with family and friends. All eyes turned to the valedictorian, escorted by Ema Davis, and to the student president of the Knights of Ilamar Book Club, which had been founded the previous fall.

After a few preliminary speeches from both the superintendent and Principal Butler—who'd taken over for Mrs. Jenkins a year and a half earlier—the MC announced: "And now, for a special word from a very special student. A diligent scholar, avid reader, and loyal friend, she was overwhelmingly elected valedictorian for her determination, her academic rigor, and her strength of character in the face of seemingly daunting odds. Ladies and gentlemen, the valedictorian for the class of 2026: Christie Charity Cunningham!"

The stadium erupted with applause. Michael Stroud led her from her seat near the front to the podium and handed her a thin volume. She opened it, placed it on the stand, traced the first few lines with her fingers, and, after a steadying breath, began:

"Good morning!" Many in the crowd returned the greeting. "It is truly an honor to stand before you today. If you had told me two years ago that I'd be here as your valedictorian, I never would have believed you. I am so deeply grateful to Jesus Christ, my Lord and Savior, for providing me with this opportunity; to Ema Davis, who led me to Him and has been a faithful guide and advocate for me; and of course to my family and loved ones—including Michael Stroud, Zechariah Forshaw, and Deputy Richard Gaines and Marie Gaines—for being there every step of the way. Thank you, from the bottom of my heart." She paused for applause. "During my time at Odessa High, I've learned three important lessons about life and about myself that I would like to share today: first, the best moments are rarely planned and often arrive in unexpected ways; second, if you need help, never be too afraid to ask for it; and third, always let God lead you—even when it's hard—or fun." Some people laughed. "This will all make sense soon, I promise."

She lifted her chin. "First, let me explain how one of the best moments in my life came about through the worst day of my life. For context, everyone who knows me knows I'm a planner by nature. I've always built my schedules, goals, and aspirations like towers of Jenga blocks. I'd scramble to adjust if even one piece shifted. But I did not plan for everything. I knew my eyesight would get worse, yet I refused to do the one thing that would have helped most: learning Braille. Pride, stubbornness, and my aversion to asking for help blinded me more than my condition ever could.

"By junior year, my vision deteriorated so quickly that I couldn't see the board from a few feet away. Suddenly, the world I loved—reading, writing, researching, studying—was gone. And I believed that it was all by my own hand, my own stubbornness, my own refusal to seek help, even when it was hard.

"But in the dark hour of my soul, the boy who had been the bane of my existence—the one who teased, talked, and snickered endlessly—*sorry, hon*—came to my aid. He had already started to change since giving his life to Christ, but that day he came through in a way I'll never forget. When I finally stopped wallowing in self-pity, I learned that he was willing to learn Braille—*blindfolded*—*with me!* Now *that's* a green flag that even *I* could spot!"

The audience laughed.

"I never could have scripted that. At first, I still resisted Braille, even after losing my functional vision. But seeing the boy who had once been the biggest thorn in my side humble himself to help me in a way that I hadn't helped myself convicted me deeply. And it worked! A year and a half ago, I couldn't read a single dot. Today, I've read Mr. Stroud's latest novel, *The Stone of Ilamar*, in Braille three times. And now, I'm headed to college to teach *other* kids how to read Braille, so they can discover the joy I found. God turned my hopelessness into His glory.

"But I also had to take personal responsibility, which

leads to my second lesson: if you need help, ask. So many people—whether struggling with physical, mental, or social difficulties—never ask for help. Sometimes it's pride, sometimes embarrassment, sometimes fear of being labeled dependent. And sometimes, they just don't know how. I was blessed with family and friends who encouraged me—dare I say *pushed* me—to advocate for myself. After going legally blind, I needed more help than ever. A teacher aide read aloud and scribed for me, and fellow classmates, family, and Mr. Stroud all pitched in with homework. I learned to use a Braille note-taker and audible computer screen reader, which gave me independence. But none of that would have happened if I hadn't asked. The answer is always no if you never ask."

She drew a deep breath. "Through it all, the Lord was faithful, even when I doubted. I had to learn to trust Him always. I learned to step out into things I never imagined: I went to the Winter Formal—and came back with a boyfriend." *Applause.* "We sought out self-defense lessons, and now, I no longer feel vulnerable when I'm alone. I lived away from my family for three weeks, and returned with new skills, greater confidence in my ability to live independently, and a better idea of where I needed to improve. It wasn't easy, but it was worth it. Through green pastures and dark valleys alike, Jesus Christ has been my Shepherd. God was faithful—always.

"So, to the classes that follow, I leave you with this: trust God, advocate for yourself, and don't allow your situation to confine your imagination. As Mike Stroud always says, your imagination is limited only by your attitude and whatever you allow between your ears. When I trusted in God, *His* love fanned my faith into flame, stirring my imagination, leading me to trust Him in all new things, which ultimately brought me to this moment before you now. As Jesus told His disciples in Matthew 6:33–34, 'But seek first the kingdom of God and His righteousness, and all these things will be added to you. Therefore do not worry about tomorrow, for tomorrow will worry about itself. Sufficient for the day is its own trouble.' His plans may not look glamorous, and they almost *certainly* won't be easy. But *His* plans are *far* greater than anything we can ever hope or imagine. So when life feels overwhelming, don't just look around, and don't look in. Look up. Thank you."

The stadium thundered with applause. The ceremony continued, but Zech and Christie allowed themselves to imagine the possibilities ahead. Zech envisioned himself teaching high school English, guiding students like Benjamin Davis— Jonathan and Ema's little boy, not even a year old now, yet already brimming with potential. Christie imagined herself helping struggling students regain power, confidence, and independence, rediscovering the joy of reading as she had. And both of them prayed the other would be by their side—two hearts shaping a love story Odessa hadn't seen in generations. As far as they were concerned, their adventures together had only just begun.

ACKNOWLEDGMENTS

I could not be more grateful to all the people who helped and encouraged me throughout the process of writing, revising, and publishing this novel. First, I thank my Heavenly Father, from whom all things come; my Lord and Savior, Jesus the Messiah, for His sacrificial, atoning death on the cross and His glorious resurrection; and the Holy Spirit of truth, Who brooded over creation and indwells all God's chosen ones. Thank You, Lord, for Your love, Your mercy, and Your creativity.

I am also deeply indebted to my beautiful girlfriend, MaKenzie, who supported, inspired, and encouraged me throughout this entire process. It was because she believed this book could be published that I found the confidence to move forward. Christie Cunningham is, in some ways, little more than a pale imitation of her. I love you, dear.

I would also like to extend my gratitude to Felicity Fox—my editor, publisher, and project manager—for so eagerly accepting this task and for guiding me through every step of the process. My thanks as well to my parents for supporting and supplying me through it all in more ways than one.

My gratitude also goes to the Summer Orientation & Mobility and Adaptive Living Resource program (S.O.A.R.), a major outreach center of Lighthouse for the Blind in the St. Louis, Missouri, area. The passing reference to a training program in Missouri was a shout-out to them, and I am grateful to Kevin Hollinger, president of the program, for allowing me to mention them as I have. I recommend that any blind youth aged sixteen through twenty-one who wish to increase their independent-living skills—or at least gain a clearer understanding of where they may need growth—consider applying. I attended in June 2025, and it was a life-changing experience, as I am sure it will be for any who do likewise.

This book was inspired in large part by Focus on the Family's esteemed radio series *Adventures in Odyssey*. I was especially reflecting on the more episodic, adventure-based episodes of the late 1980s and early 1990s, juxtaposed with the more plot- or character-driven arcs of the late 2000s onward. Each has its merits—indeed, arcs such as "The Blackgaard Chronicles" and "The Green Ring Conspiracy" can and do contain riveting plots. Still, there was something almost magical—if that is the right word—about some of the shorter arcs, like the adventures the kids at Whit's End would take in the Imagination Station (which inspired the Dark Room), and Whit's mysterious, gently coaxing way of encouraging them to explore their questions through Scripture and imagination. (From this, I am sure you can guess which character was inspired.) So, for what it's worth, thank you, *Odyssey*, for inspiring Odessa and so much more.

The title of this book is, as Michael Stroud puts it, a play on words—*imagination, Imagine Nation*. The book he references is a real children's story I remember hearing at a book club, featuring a jolly old man named Chris Cringle who genuinely believes he is Santa Claus and helps a cynical little girl reawaken her sense of wonder, invoking the same wordplay Mike uses in my story. Tragically, I cannot remember the book's title or its publication date, so if my chronology is off—Mike opened the store under the name *Imagine Nation* in 1987—I apologize and ask for your grace.

I could go on, but this is meant to be a list of thanks rather than a collection of Easter eggs. So thank you—each one of you—for joining me on this adventure, whether as producer, endorser, or reader. I hope that this book, no matter your background or disposition, challenges, entertains, and encourages you in whatever way you need to grow. Jewish, Christian, atheist—all: welcome to *Imagine Nation.*

Soli Deo gloria!

ABOUT THE AUTHOR

Caiden Hooks is not your typical college senior. He has been tackling his college experience like a wrestler hitting the food table after making weight. With graduation on the horizon, he will be celebrating obtaining his degree Summa Cum Laude, including a double major and triple minors—all while serving as a successful four-year mainstay on the college wrestling team.

Oh, and did I mention Caiden is also blind—totally blind? Both of his eyes were removed in childhood to save his life following a three-year battle with aggressive eye cancer. Yet being blind is merely a fact, and Caiden refuses to let it define him. One might assume losing your vision in grade school would have slowed him down; but you would be seriously mistaken. Losing his eyesight proved to be only a bump in the road. Caiden now sees the world through a unique lens—one free from the constant visual distractions that overwhelm the rest of us. His writing reflects this perspective in the depth and breadth of his descriptions and in the spirited journeys of his characters.

While Caiden is not quite a New York Times

bestseller—yet—his wholesome storytelling and boundless imagination make it easy to root for him to join the list one day.

When he is not writing, Caiden can be found around campus in his Otterbein Wrestling gear, heading to class, to wrestling practice, to play the piano, or to sing with the campus Christian Fellowship group, and on occasion even performing the National Anthem to open sporting events, sometimes for his own team's dual meets.

Get to know this inspiring young author. You are sure to enjoy his heartwarming adventures. This book is just the beginning—a springboard for many more incredible journeys to come.